APEX

E.M. Miller

Black Rose Writing | Texas

©2021 by E.M. Miller
All rights reserved. No part of this book may be reproduced, stored in a retrieval system or transmitted in any form or by any means without the prior written permission of the publishers, except by a reviewer who may quote brief passages in a review to be printed in a newspaper, magazine or journal.

The author grants the final approval for this literary material.

First printing

This is a work of fiction. Names, characters, businesses, places, events, and incidents are either the products of the author's imagination or used in a fictitious manner. Any resemblance to actual persons, living or dead, or actual events is purely coincidental.

Content includes mature themes such as sex, violence, murder, sexual assault, large volumes of gore, and the use of firearms and other weapons.

ISBN: 978-1-68433-872-6
PUBLISHED BY BLACK ROSE WRITING
www.blackrosewriting.com

Printed in the United States of America
Suggested Retail Price (SRP) $17.95

Apex is printed in Caslon

*As a planet-friendly publisher, Black Rose Writing does its best to eliminate unnecessary waste to reduce paper usage and energy costs, while never compromising the reading experience. As a result, the final word count vs. page count may not meet common expectations.

To the mother that raised me to be unbreakable, willful, and unrepentantly complicated.

To my baby sister, for whom I will be strong until my dying breath.

To the community and family of brilliant and powerful women that taught me what it means to be such.

To the ladies that are liberated by their multifaceted souls.

To the people that revel in their secrets.

And most importantly, to my father, may he rest in peace.

APEX

apex predator : noun
/ˈāpeks/ /ˈpredədər/

Definition of apex predator ecology : a predator at the top of a food chain that is not preyed upon by any other animal

PROLOGUE

The crinkle of damaged speakers croaking out country music followed him out of the bar. A blue glow descended on the chipped, concrete steps. His heart thumped hard with the anticipation of what he was about to do. He'd had his eye on her all night. She'd looked confused, weary, starving for something different. Girls like that don't know what they want until it's given to them, and his favorite hobby was doing just that. Women like to play coy, lead men on a little chase, and he was no fool. He always caught them, and if they didn't want to be caught, they wouldn't let him.

A part of him had a stomach specifically reserved for churning when he knew something wasn't considered right. It was distant, but it existed, and he almost let it get to him sometimes. But another, stronger part of him was hungry, and it drowned out the conscience that most people were ruled by. A feeling that strong couldn't be wrong, he figured. Looking at the girl opening her truck door, that hunger flared. Her skirt hinted at something shapely beneath, and her little, scuffed heels on her feet would make it harder to run. That was a shame. He kind of liked it when they ran.

"Hey, little miss," he drawled, tucking his dip behind his back molars.

She turned, and he almost hissed aloud in satisfaction. Her face was open, eyes wide with innocence. The natural submission in her gaze nearly snapped his control in half before he had a chance to play his game.

"I noticed you all alone in there, you lookin' to meet someone special?"

She cocked her head. Her exposed throat looked smooth and clean; young skin. His tongue darted out to wet his lips.

"I'm just passing through the area," she replied, her soft voice wavering a bit. She gave an unsure smile. "I thought I'd stop in for a bit of a break from the road."

"Aw, you a little tired, sweetheart?"

"Actually, yes, I've been traveling for quite a while…"

"Where you headin'?"

"Back west. I'm movin' into my daddy's house."

"Well, miss, if you give me some company tonight, I can offer you some rest from the road," he crooned, coming in closer and resting an arm on the truck.

She angled herself away from him a bit, blushing prettily. She busied herself with something in the backseat, avoiding a response.

"Come on now, honey, you were lookin' pretty lonely in there, I'm just tryin' to help you out."

"I don't know, I should probably get back on the road," she said, casting him a bashful smile.

He reached out and drew a finger from her shoulder down to her elbow. She tucked her arm against herself, looking downwards. Anger flared in him. The prudish little bitch. As if she hadn't been trying to entice him with her coquettish behavior. She needed to be taught what her flirting would get her.

"Why don't you give me a minute to show you-"

He reached out, gripping her upper arm. She squirmed against him, and something flashed in her eyes. Not quite fear, but something else. Something like…readiness.

He found himself wrapping both arms around her to keep her from wrestling out of his grasp.

"Fiery little bitch," he bit out, pushing her towards her open backseat door. He maneuvered her slight body over the floor of her lifted vehicle, feeling victorious but a bit uneasy. Despite his sudden attack, the young woman didn't struggle much or make any noise. Part of him wondered why, but his hunger overrode the flicker of doubt.

Reaching between them, he fumbled one-handed with his zipper, keeping a firm grasp on her delicate wrists with the other hand. As he pulled the tab down and prepared to push up her layered skirt, he heard her finally utter a sound. He thought he recognized the syllables that fell out of her mouth, but he had to be wrong. A chill ran up his spine, quelching his hunger immediately.

"What did you just say?" he asked gruffly, trying to conceal his distress.

Her words came out on one breath, "Victor Baker."

His breath hitched, and for a moment, he lost his grip on her. That moment was long enough for her to whip one hand out of his grasp and pull a pipe out from under the seat. She whirled with a speed he didn't expect and swung the pipe into his temple. Victor crumpled to the ground, and the young woman stood over him for a beat, gazing down at the pile of unwashed clothes and sweat-slicked flesh. His forehead bore a white-rapidly-turning-red mark, and a fluttering began in her stomach.

• • •

Jane always felt the flap of wings inside when her scenes began. The foreplay of subterfuge was at best amusing; the real hunt began when she made the first move. She felt her blood pounding hot in her ears as she removed the chains she'd prepared from her backseat. She tsked to herself at not having attached the spring clips beneath the hitch ahead of time. Efficiency was everything. She would make a note for herself next time.

Crossing the chains around and under Victor's arms, she grunted as she lifted his dead weight to lock the clips into place behind him, lest he regain consciousness as she dragged him behind the truck. She handcuffed him with a flourish, as if tying the bow atop a Christmas present. Her finished work was beautiful, just a bit of blood, nothing that would stand out amongst the traces of bar brawls amongst the gravel and broken glass of the parking lot. It wasn't finished, though. She still had some finishing touches to make.

Jane started up her truck and made sure the radio was still all static, silently thanking the radio jammer sitting atop her console that faithfully prevented any security footage of her escapades- not that she suspected the cameras actually worked. The bar was perfect for her hobby: isolated and the site of too many expected crimes to be suspicious in a way that drew attention to her. She was truly blessed that her new friend, Victor, happened to frequent the establishment. She hummed to herself as she pondered her good luck. *People sure have loose tongues around here,* she thought. *I didn't even need* a database to find him. She also suspected that no one would look too deeply into Victor's upcoming accident.

Pulling out of the bar, Jane prepared to switch off the jammer and play her favorite tape. Every time "Runaround Sue" played, Jane felt as if she were hearing it for the first time all over again. She crooned along to Dion DiMucci's addictive notes, drowning out the sound of a suddenly very awake Victor, who was just discovering his unfortunate situation. Despite her bliss at accomplishing yet another scene, a deep, dark stirring began in her chest at the distant sounds of Victor's pained howls.

He deserves this.

Victor Baker spent his time bumming drugs off of friends and finding vulnerable women to confirm what he thinks of himself. His reputation started out as a bit of a cad as a young buck, and rapidly declined into that of a full-on predator. Not many went about town with Victor these days, she'd heard, because he was the kind to follow girls into dark places when they weren't looking, and made sure to always be a couple drinks behind them. He was the perfect monster to quench her thirst in the midst of her travels.

Victor hollered a couple miles more, but Jane had made sure to leave the chain long enough that his head reached the road despite the angle and the speed of the vehicle. His weight wasn't enough to pull the chain taught, and instead, he flopped about in the rear-view mirror, going silent as she sped up. Jane grinned a mirthless grin, and hummed the last few notes of her favorite song.

After arriving at the creek, which lay deep in a bed far below the bridge she was parked on, she tossed the chain to the other side of the narrow bed and reattached it with practiced hands.

Jane did it the way an artist cleans up her materials after painting a masterpiece.

Jane took her bike out of the back of her car and sped back up the road to the bar.

An artist removes her painting from the scene of elegant, acrylic destruction.

Jane tossed the bike in the back of Victor's dusty pick up.

The artist brings her brushes to a sink, removing them from their jars and pallets.

Jane drives the truck back to the creek, and uses Victor's chains to lever him into the front seat.

The artist lovingly massages the paint from her brushes, using soft suds and warm water to keep the pigment from creeping up to the wood.

Jane uses a rock to smash in the windshield and pulls Victor through the artfully-created hole.

The artist sets the brushes aside to dry, and removes her rags to be washed with her destroyed clothes.

Jane detaches the chains and gives the gas pedal a nudge, quickly flitting out of the way, to send the truck careening over the edge of the bank and into the creek with a deafening crash.

The artist beams at their finished work from across the room, satisfied with the outcome.

Jane watches the water rush over the rapidly sinking vehicle, Victor's prostrate form at an awkward angle on the hood of the car.

Both artists walk away from their work with a contented sigh.

CHAPTER 1

Golden Eagle, Aquila chrysaetos

Jane took in a deep breath and exhaled into the air, searching for that misty cloud that used to appear in Louisiana, the one that played with the humidity in the early morning air, comparing, toying, and finally, dissipating. Here in West Texas, however, smack in the middle of the desert, her breath fell flat, not a trace of it to be found clinging to the soup that used to be her environment.

It's not that Jane wasn't glad to be home, she was in a way, but she knew that with the move would come questions and complications, as well as the distasteful activity of establishing a reputation in order to avoid being detected. It helped that she naturally looked sweet, and was just interesting enough in public not to draw attention to her pristine demeanor. One must have a bit of dust on the carpet to keep people from looking for the piles of dirt underneath.

However, establishing herself as a Good Girl and a Law Abiding Citizen meant that she would need to hold off on her hobby for a little while. No scenes while she was in the process of reintroducing herself to her old hometown.

At that thought, she frowned up at the ceiling of her front porch.

The creaking porch swing swayed to and fro, and she looked up at the moving slat board above her. Sitting on this swing with her father was one of the many cherished memories she had of her childhood here. No amount of gory endings could erase what she knew about her family.

Her mother, although deceased by the time Jane was self-aware, was said to be the loveliest and gentlest of her brood. Her sisters all had one thing or another wrong with them; gapped teeth, a screeching voice, limp hair, one leg shorter than the other...but Jane's mother was perfect. At least that's what she heard from everyone in town. Her father never refuted the claims, but chose to emphasize other traits to his daughter.

"Janie, your mother was the most clever creature I ever met. Besides myself of course." And here he would wink, and Jane would giggle at her humble father's rare mention of his intelligence. "She could whip up an answer to any question I had, and she always knew where everything was, right down to a thumbtack. Your mama had golden hair like yours, but a little less red, and every time she would flash those green eyes at me, and toss that hair, I knew she was lookin' for a kiss."

Jane would take this moment to stick her finger in her mouth and gag.

"She hated that my job isn't safe, but she knew things, just like you know things. She knew how important it was for the town to be safe, even if I wasn't always safe."

Jane always pursed her lips at the mention of her father's dangerous career. She chose to think of police work as daring and exciting, something that she and her father bonded over. However, a little niggle in her brain would remind her every now and then that he put his life on the line for his community fairly often. That niggle would turn into a frantic writhing when he was late coming home, or when she heard about a violent criminal on the radio. That didn't keep her from desperately wanting to follow in his footsteps.

Sitting up and swinging her feet onto the rough, unfinished porch, Jane shook the memories out of her ears before they led to something upsetting.

Time to get to work.

Creating a personality that enfolds her into the arms of a community was only ever as difficult as the formula she chose. Sometimes she was shy and easily shaken. Occasionally, she would be a bubbly, green gal who giggled when she was nervous. She was always vulnerable, and never overly aware.

The difficult part this time would be recreating a personality amongst people that already knew her.

Once upon a time, Jane lived with her father in this sturdy, desert-creek-side bungalow with two hounds that slept on the porch, and the memories of her mother blanketing every surface. Detective Fairweather was put on a pedestal by the community long before his death, and the trust that he had instilled in everyone lingered in his young daughter. There was no shortage of peers who wanted to take Jane in when she was orphaned, but unfortunately, that's not the way the foster system operates. Her small town was insignificant enough to escape a place on a map, and was most certainly not considered a suitable location for her to live when the incident occurred. A town rife with murder hardly warrented the trust of Child Protective Services.

Fort Zemsta was a remnant of Old West, outlaws and corrupt law enforcement echoing in the fibers of the community like a ghost that refused to be forgotten. Her father was a litmus test for those who were up to no good- if a man trusted Detective Fairweather and treated him well, then he was a law-abiding citizen. If a man kept one eye on him and didn't take well to his presence...one could ascertain that such a man had a sinister reason for doing so.

At the time of her father's death, Jane had been just old enough yet just impressionable enough to have a strong opinion about leaving her home town, and she did little to hide it from her foster parents. At every opportunity, the young woman would sneak away from her, at best, negligent foster families to find a route back home. Unfortunately, her youth and inexperience thwarted her at every turn. It wasn't until she was a hardened, jaded foster child, void of any remaining identity as a loved daughter, that she changed her tactics.

Jane couldn't truthfully say that her foster experience had been without any kind of comfort- the occasional foster mother or father would possess good intentions and do everything possible to right the wrongs of Jane's past. Jane wearily but readily accepted their love and assistance until the inevitable time arrived that it would be snatched from her and drowned in the sea of paperwork and new faces that spoke the same words. It would start out sickly sweet, eerily familiar... and then everything would fall apart.

It was best to stay prepared, she'd learned, as even the worst of monsters could hide behind a smile and a shallow background check. Had her father's death not scarred her permanently, the foster system would have effectively finished the job.

Perhaps I don't need an intricate character after all, she thought, pacing through the house, stalling before she prepared for the day.

She may have been a child here, but the citizens of Fort Zemsta couldn't possibly expect anything in particular from a victim of loss and abuse. This was one instance in which she could attempt to be herself, or rather, a socially acceptable variant of that. She mulled over the thought, dressing with such a theme in mind.

Who exactly was Jane Fairweather?

Typically, when preparing for a scene in a new location, the first impression required every detail to be thoroughly thought-out. Her costumes were chosen and worn with precision, but today would be different. This would not be the town's first impression of Jane, but rather, the grand premier of her adult self. What does one wear to a grand premier?

Jane decided that an imitation of childlike whimsy with a nod to her adult figure would be her best chance at developing an immediate sense of connection between the townspeople and whom they believed her to be.

Or rather, whom she would have them believe her to be.

On her tip-toes, Jane rifled through the high shelf where a few of her mother's belongings had been left by the previous owner. Thankfully, not many of the superstitious townspeople had attempted to move anything when the house became deserted, and even new owners left things like this where they belonged.

A cloud of peach-colored thread caught Jane's eye, and she extracted it carefully, unraveling the item with reverent fingers.

Her mother's favorite, knit cardigan was in perfect shape, preserved by the small, worn trunk where many of her belongings resided. It had been a birthday gift from tiny Jane, aided by her father as they searched stores on the strip for something that befit Claire Fairweather's sentimental nature with a lightness belonging in a desert. She knew the sweater to be a time capsule of her mother's scent, and as she gathered the material in her hands, she hesitantly brought it to her face and did something quite uncharacteristic. Closing her eyes, she inhaled deeply, taking in the faint wisps of jasmine and something else, something that smelt like a mixture of hot clay and cooking, maybe something baking, maybe freshly tilled soil. Things that were intrinsic to the vision Jane held in her mind of her mother, things that would never disappear.

A very small part of her felt a twinge of remorse at using something so sacred as a part of her charade, but as she recalled the purpose for it, the remorse toppled over and fell into a deep pit of unending indignation at the injustice that her other parent faced in this town.

Her eyes opened and refocused, and she tossed the cardigan on the bed with the other items of clothing she'd chosen. Opening the Crosley record player she'd unpacked in her bedroom, she placed a carefully-chosen vinyl disc over the center spindle and dropped the needle. Dion's voice followed the endearing crackle, and Jane lifted up on the balls of her feet to bounce to the beat as she prepared.

"Here's my story, it's sad but true…"

She swept her hair off her face and pulled it back with a ribbon from around one of the packages she'd purchased on her way into town. The satin sheen wove from the ribbon into her hair, and her locks became a halo around her blank face. Staring into her vanity mirror, she practiced her smiles, giving each of her best ones in order of how she invented them.

"Now listen people what I'm tellin' you…"

The mirror framed a frozen picture as she stopped on the one she'd chosen. Her dimples bracketed her upturned lips, opened just wide enough to show off the rounded teeth in front, concealing the sharper, more ominous ones on the sides. Sweet as sugar, but with an aftertaste of almonds…

"A-keep away from Runaround Sue."

• • •

"Aaah, she likes to travel around, yeah! She'll love you and she'll put you down-"

The Ford rumbled to a stop as Facundo turned the key, and Dion and the Belmonts cut off. The dust swirling up from his tires settled, clearing just enough for the facade of the old building to become clear through the streaked windshield.

The list of "pros" for owning a bar starts with "#1- late opening hours". At one in the afternoon, coming back from mass, Facundo knew that he would be walking into a clean building, chairs turned over neatly on the surface of the tables, and the air would be stiff with the welcoming smell of still liquor until he turned on the AC. Of all the mistakes, misunderstandings, and misadventures in his life, this bar was one of the outlying positives- a beacon at the end of a very long tunnel.

The Red Light welcomed visitors with the homey facade of the old public library- small, worn, and safe. The library had been cramped and rarely visited, but it was one of the rare places in the poor town that people could visit without the expectation of spending their sparse change. Higher education wasn't widely regarded as necessary in Fort Zemsta, but that didn't mean the townspeople didn't have an appreciation for literature of any kind. Many of the texts (particularly the legal ones) were affectionately dog-eared and bookmarked, and they had the appearance of once being treasured enough that Facundo couldn't bear to ship them away or dispose of them. It was for that reason that they continued to reside within the walls of the building.

The name of the bar came from the well-known fact that late in the evening, the original librarian of the building would leave her lamp on in her office, which would shine through the sheer, burgundy curtains onto the street below. It was a smoke signal, a watchtower, a lighthouse, to passing folks that the library was welcome even in the unfriendly hours of the night when the streets felt unfamiliar. The light gave off a red hue, which made you want to stop in your tracks and turn in. The librarian that replaced her just before it stopped receiving sufficient funding made it slightly less welcome, but preserved its charm.

Many had advised the man to name it after his most common moniker to indicate that it was his- "Cundo's", but the current occupants were nevertheless fond of the instant hang out spot that their old buddy provided. Though his life was much slower now that he was a medically retired vet, the scars on his body, visible and often frightening to others, were a constant physical reminder of who he used to be.

He shook the thought of his scars off and with a flick of his thumb, Facundo brought the jukebox to life across the bar, using the bluetooth connection on his phone to continue the song he'd been enjoying in the truck.

His mother had been fond of older music, doo wop and swing, softer, gentler rock like Dion, and she often led her young son on pilgrimages to museums and memorials to The Greats across the states.

"If something has been loved this long, it's earned its place in the present," she would say, and surrender to the warbling voices of the past with a serene smile on her face.

Cundo looked back on those moments fondly, but always wondered if his mother's innocence had been a factor in her demise. He knew enough to know, however, that blaming a victim's fate on his or her character traits was always a mistake. Life is infinitely simpler as a civilian, when you feel less compelled to unearth the motives of everyone around you. That didn't always stop him, but there were certain things that nailed the coffin of his life as a member of the Marine Corps shut and opened windows to other parts of his being.

One of those moments had just walked through the door.

The unsuspecting bar owner was lowering the last chair to the floor and wiping his palms on his dark-wash jeans when she breezed through the threshold. Somehow, without him seeing, she'd waved a magic wand and frozen everything around her in time, including the stunned and sole occupant of the room, who now watched her move in stupefaction.

The creature before him seemed to defy the air around her, which was usually clouded slightly with desert dust, but was now crystal clear aside from the warm halo around her. Cocooned in a soft sweater, long skirt, and little, pink shoes, the whole of her was tied off with a satin ribbon atop her head, pulling back masses of red-gold curls. Cundo was hardly able to pull his eyes away from the flames of her hair, but lowered his gaze to take in the girl's out-of-place expression. While she appeared untouched, glazed in an immaculate kind of grace from head-to-toe, the look on her face was one of slight, disdainful boredom. Her rosebud lips curled at the sight of the shelves against the walls, and despite the spell she'd cast on Cundo, he felt a prickle of warning on the back of his neck. His confusion grew when her gaze landed on him and transformed so completely, that he was taken aback.

Venomous but relaxed at first, she'd looked like a serpent lazily making her way into a new den of prey. All of the sudden, though, her expression melted into one of wide-eyed, innocent bewilderment, and her pursed lips fell open, softening, as if she were a black-and-white movie star that had just discovered a secret worthy of a swoon. Typically, Cundo would have assumed that the expression was due to her taking in his face for the first time, but it looked too calculated, and she didn't seem to be in a hurry to look away.

Her new prey, for that's how Cundo felt, involuntarily took a step back when she proceeded forward, her small feet gliding on the contrasting floor, scuffed and mottled with the boots of regular customers. She smiled nervously, deep dimples appearing on either side of her pink-lemonade-lips, as if she had something to say, but wasn't sure if she should.

"Hey, there," she spoke, and Cundo was instantly back under the spell. If fairies spoke, their voices sounded like this. "I s'pose you just opened, I'm so sorry to bother you."

He simply stood, still frozen, feeling as though he may never move again.

"I'm new...well, sorta, and I just wanted to swing by my old favorite place, but it...it seems as if..."

She trailed off, glancing about the first floor of the building. When her bell-like voice faded into silence, and she began biting her bottom lip, Cundo finally unfroze.

"I'm sorry you didn't hear, but the library is a bar now," he surprised himself with an even voice. "How are you sort of new?"

"What's that?" she responded distractedly, though for some reason, he got the impression that she knew exactly what he'd just said.

"How are you sort of new, did you just move back?"

"Oh, yes," she breathed wistfully, adopting a sad smile, again looking like an actress from a black-and-white movie. Lucille Ball came to mind. "I moved home to buy my daddy's old cabin back. It went back up for sale, and I couldn't resist." The dimples returned.

He reached out with a hand that felt steadier than the rest of him, and shook her much smaller, much softer one. He noticed that she stared at his hand for a moment before taking it.

"Cundo," he stated abruptly, his name sounding ridiculous in his ears as he introduced himself, unsolicited. She nodded with a closed-lipped smile, not returning with her name. He added that to his mental list.

"Who was your father?" Cundo asked without preamble. There wasn't a single stranger in Fort Zemsta, and he was sure he could solve the mystery of this ethereal creature if he discovered her origins.

"Oh, you probably wouldn't remember him," she said, her bell voice belying the slightest of strains. She covered it up by ducking her head and blushing prettily. A cynical part of him wondered how she was capable of doing that on command.

"I'll find out eventually."

He didn't know why he said it, particularly in that gruff sort of way. Cundo was known to have a weak spot for women, damsels in distress especially, and had never ended a statement with anything but "ma'am" when addressing one. For some reason, though, he felt the need to be merciless with her, as if she were a perp he needed to shake in order to get answers.

Something in her eyes flickered, something like respect, or maybe exasperation. It was impossible to tell.

"Allen Fairweather."

Ice shot through his veins and recognition up his throat.

"Detective...Allen Fairweather?" he asked tentatively.

She nodded curtly, dropping her pretty-in-pink veil for just a moment. He could understand why. Detective Fairweather had been the town's one and only detective for quite a while, and every ear in town had been told the tale of his gruesome end. His was one of those tragic deaths that was talked about, and one of the few times that the townspeople didn't protect one of their many criminals. Everyone had loved Fairweather, he'd been a pillar of the community in more than a few ways. His death had simply been labeled as "unjust" and would always be so...even Cundo, a non-native to the town, knew his story.

Realization dawned on him.

"You're...little Janie Fairweather?"

Her facade slipped even more, and he caught a glimpse of the coiled snake he saw earlier.

"Yes," she almost hissed, but just as quickly regained her composure while placing her small, leather bag on the table beside her. He eyed it, something about the bag registering as familiar. "I miss him of course, and I thought it was about time I came back home. To...honor his memory."

Something felt off about the way the Fairweather girl said everything, but he sensed the sincerity in her grief. He'd seen it many times before. Felt it. His instincts told him not to press the subject further.

"Well, I'm sure they're glad to have you back. What brings you by the library first thing?" he said, trying to sound nonchalant, moving behind the bar to open the cash register. She followed his movements, hands twitching along the bar's glossy surface as if it were the first bartop she'd ever seen.

"The library is...important to me. I used to spend a lot of time there as a kid," she whispered with genuine fondness, her gaze lingering on the shelves to the right of the room that cradled the second floor landing. She glanced up at the loft, her eyes following the steel access ladder that led to it, and incidentally, his living space. A wave of heat rolled through him as he wondered what she was thinking.

"I'm sorry to disappoint, but the library is still available for lending. Anyone who comes in is free to read while they dine or have a few beers… or more, ha. Customers can borrow the books as long as they return them in a few days, I don't mind," he croaked on the last word, hoping that he didn't sound like a babbling idiot. Luckily, as a former local, she would understand the absurd trust that the people of Zemsta had for one another. Tourists and criminals were both delighted by it, but locals knew that where there were unlocked doors, there were also gun-toting owners and local officers that turned a blind eye to outlaw justice.

Shoving his hands in his jeans pockets to keep them from lifting in the air and making gestures as idiotic as his rambling, he turned to look out at the shelves. She followed his gaze and her dimples appeared, bracketing a snow-white smile.

"That sounds lovely. I'll have to come by and order a uh- what's something the regulars like?"

"That'd have to be my famous pulled pork nachos with an ice-cold prickly pear margarita," he stated, a hint of pride coloring his gruff voice. He smoked the pork himself, and made all of the simple syrups for signature drinks in his own kitchen upstairs.

"Mmmm, that sounds like the pick-me-up a girl needs after a long day," she quipped, a twinkle in her eye. He imagined that despite her slight form, she had enough hidden fire to put away serious liquor. He wondered once again how she was continuing to look at him without wincing at this face.

"I'll have to swing on by later this evening after I get a good look at all the new changes," she said, her voice pulled taut. "There are so many."

He waved weakly at her retreating form, unable to come up with a substantial goodbye. Two feelings warred inside him- the desperate desire to have her back in his place of residence this evening, and the ominous feeling that trouble might follow this woman into his bar.

As he watched the door close behind her, his mind caught up with the rest of him and gave a nudging reminder as to where he'd seen her familiar-looking purse before. It was a purse made for carrying a concealed weapon.

Hm. Once a local, always a local, I suppose.

• • •

She walked briskly back to her truck, practically spitting at the ground as she kicked up dust in the once-familiar parking lot. The second she pulled up to the building, she knew it had been transformed from the place she'd adored, but to see the interior, the shelves she'd once disappeared between for hours on end, pushed back against the walls, as decorations, to make room for unwashed, illiterate masses to swarm the place and dirty it...she felt as though she'd been personally assaulted. The library had once been not only a safe haven for her, but for her mother as well. She would stay all night restocking the shelves, organizing the card catalogues, and splaying out new magazines and pamphlets on the tables to interest people who simply needed a place to sit for a while. As the librarian, the first Jane had ever known, and the last that she wished to, Claire Fairweather had been a mother to anyone that walked in the door. Now, the door led to a bar. A type of establishment that Jane typically used as a hunting ground.

She'd wanted to ground herself in memories before starting her search, to make it personal instead of the distant kind of game she usually played. Rather, she found a skeleton of her second home, and a neandertal in dusty boots parading around inside of it.

Slamming the car door behind her as she climbed in, she looked up at the metal sign hanging above the door.

"The Red Light".

Ha. Cute.

CHAPTER 2

The King Cobra, Ophiophagus hannah

Jane had planned to spend the day making strategic errands to make herself known and establish that she was back in town, all grown up but still the same innocent, trusting child from years ago. Her list had included a boutique that a friend of her mother's owned, the post office, the local market, and the small hardware store that resided near The Red Light.

Pulling back into the parking lot she'd peeled out of earlier, she snorted at the memory of the disheveled man this morning. He'd appeared confused by the sight of her, but in a rather pleasing way. Although she couldn't relate to the sensation, she knew that men experienced it when she was near. She appeared delicate, in that way men seem to like, and her fair, clear complexion was an easy mask to hide behind. Men never questioned why someone too young and too pure would show up in their filthy, ramshackle whereabouts, they simply lunged from their caves like a sea worm trying to suck prey back into their dwellings. Men never questioned. That was their downfall.

Somehow, this "Soon-doh" or "Cuhn-dough" man seemed less clueless than most civilian men she met. His eye was sharp, and when they roamed over her figure, as per male protocol, he seemed to be searching for something specific.

Jane was never one to take interest in people sexually. Whatever gene or bone or gland or virus made people fawn over each other and look past glaring flaws for the sake of a few moments of reciprocated touching...Jane didn't have it. No one seemed worth pursuing an elongated version of what she experienced with the fumbling, sweaty boys from high school. She'd been curious as to what other teenage humans could possibly be so enamored with, seeing how bored they were with everything else. What she was met with was a duller, less alarming version of the abuse she encountered in her foster homes. Nothing at all satisfying or enlightening.

In the foster homes, the fathers, sometimes older brothers, and strangers-turned-guests, were all potential predators. After a while, Jane knew to be obedient when she met her new family, compliant. If she did everything they asked, then it would take longer for them to show their true colors. By the time she got to college and began studying psychology, she was able to discover why so many men she came across had done what they did. Why they felt entitled to her body, her dignity, her soul. When she met her first kill, she knew that she'd gained an understanding of the predator's mindset for a reason- to become one.

But "Soone-Dowe" didn't raise her hackles the way other members of the male species did. He also seemed to know enough about her father that he could recognize his name and not jump at the opportunity to indicate he knew about his death. Perhaps the man knew more than he let on, and could aid her in her scene.

She thought about the stranger for a moment, holding an image of him in her mind's eye; his skin looked tanned and worn the way everyone's did in the desert, but he didn't have the freckles and discolouring that came with an abundance of time, or the signs of early aging that the outlaws had, the ones that moved on foot most places.

His face was olive-complected with an apricot filter, shadowed by two slashes of dark brows and even darker eyes that sunk into his face behind sharp cheekbones and thick lashes. She'd vaguely noticed some scarring on the right side of his face, but the rest of him was far too intriguing to worry about it. The set of his unyielding mouth and sculpted jaw reminded her of the Tigua people that lived not far away. Just envisioning his face gave her the queer sensation that she should visit him again, and truly follow up on the statement she'd made earlier.

Looking down at her arms as she got out of the car and into the brilliant sun, she examined the obvious differences between them. The Polish settlement in Zemsta was close to the border and smack in the middle of territories belonging to people that looked quite different from the Baltic natives that arrived, squat, rotund, and pale, in big wooden boats years ago. This development produced a race of people with thick, brown hair, dark eyes, and compact bodies that freckled but never burned. Jane's mother's family was one of those that had somehow remained quite white- married white, bred white, and stayed white. Jane always wondered what kind of cruel God would let her parents breed in West Texas, where the sun was unforgiving to fair children with red-head complexions. As she grew up, she wondered why the sun bounced off her skin like a white sheet on a clothesline while most of her classmates could run among the mountains and blend in with the layered rock behind them. Jane needed sunscreen and scarves that covered her neck and forehead on field trips, and the other kids were free to play shirtless in the sun. With her mother's family dying off and moving away by the time it was just her and her father, she had few other people to compare herself to. Few people to explain to her why she looked different.

"Zuunn-doe" had probably played apart from the other kids, she mused. He seemed like an introverted sort. She shook her head free of the intrusive thought and bounced into the hardware store with the beginnings of her grinning mask growing on her face for the cashier.

The tinkling of the door chimes brought up the bowed heads of several men at the counter. Among the weathered faces, one was fresher, and towered above the rest. Jane thought irrationally for a moment that her thoughts had conjured the man, and that he'd known she'd been thinking of him.

"Well, look who it is," drawled "Scoondow" with a tentative half-grin on his face that might've been a full one had his scars not been keeping one side in place. Jane instantly flushed with indignation, not used to being recognized.

"Yes, good afternoon. I'm so glad I caught you here," she responded with a teeth-baring smile, satisfied at his surprise. The older men looked on, amused. "I saw that you weren't in the bar, and thought a helpful gentleman in here might be able to point me in the right direction to find you. And look at that!"

She turned on her heel and walked, light-footed down the nearest aisle, leaving the men to consider what she might've needed their young friend for.

"Where did that little thing come from?" she overheard one of them whisper, the "ths" coming out as "ds" as they were wont to do in Zemsta.

"I heard Jan down at the market saying she's a townie comin' back from college," another replied.

"Nah, the college girls never come back, they marry yankees."

"You talked to her, Facundo, do you know what she wants?"

Facundo, she thought to herself. Hm.

"She's here to buy her father's house," Cundo's gravelly voice responded, settling the dispute.

"Who's her father?"

"Ain't she the old deacon's girl?"

"Allen Fairweather."

Silence.

Jane paused mid-browse behind a stand of various zip-ties, wanting desperately to hear the response.

"Oh, well that's…"

"And she's comin' back all alone?"

"Who's takin' care of her?"

Cundo huffed at the questions that were presumably directed to him. Jane huffed in synchronization at the idea of her needing to be taken care of, particularly after years of being victimized by those who were supposed to do just that. She loudly tossed materials into her small shopping basket, hoping that her frustration would travel on sound waves.

"She's grown, I can't imagine she needs takin' care of," he bit out, silencing the old men who simply grumbled and went back to scratching away at whatever they had on their gridded paper on the counter.

Jane approached the counter, her basket heavy with zip ties, hinges, Hasp locks, and screws. The old men straightened their spines in the presence of the young lady they could now identify.

"Your daddy was a good man, Miss Fairweather," said the eldest, his white mustache wiggling comically with each word.

"Thank you," she said amiably, although the mention of her father was alien to her, having grown up in towns that never knew her father. Inside, she bristled a bit, automatically wanting to defend her privacy. It would take awhile to reacclimate to the town's natural nosiness.

The eldest man, evidently the cashier at the moment, began writing the items from her basket by hand in the dusty receipt book on the counter. Jane marvelled at that for a moment, wondering how many other relics from her childhood had been preserved by the outdated town's culture.

"Here you go, missy," said White Mustache with a wink, tearing off the carbon copy and handing her receipt to her. Out of the corner of her eye, she caught Cundo staring at her strangely.

His voice caught her off-guard as she turned to go-

"Are you still planning to come to The Red Light this evening?"

"Oh, ha," she laughed girlishly in response, stalling for a moment. "Well, sure, if I haven't bugged you with my presence enough." She flashed a grin at him, and while the old men smirked in response to the exchange, Cundo looked grim. Suddenly he nodded, seeming to come to a conclusion to himself.

"Let me walk you over then."

She was about to make a surly comment in reaction to their conversation about being "taken care of", but she reminded herself that if she was going to use the locals for her scene, she couldn't let her facade fall in front of them.

"Why, thank you," she purred sweetly. For some reason, this made him frown.

Outside, in the bright June light, her sweater felt suffocating, but she kept a pleasant smile on her face as she attempted mindless chatter with her silent walking partner. He dwarfed her standing next to her, making her chest tight as she tried to appear carefree. Her body was always prepared to defend herself against much larger men, especially when she was "onstage", but for some reason, her defenses felt weak, unprepared, in front of this man. Perhaps it was the way he looked lost in thought, not locked in on her with a predator's focus.

"I'm glad you decided to come back this evening," he said quietly, his voice like rocks tumbling over each other down the mountains. She tensed.

"Well, you didn't leave me much of a choice," she attempted to sound humorous. "You set up shop right in the middle of my favorite place."

"I'm truly sorry about that." He did sound sorry.

"Well, if my books are going to be read somewhere other than a library, I suppose it should be in a bar, my second favorite place," she joked.

He furrowed his brow, his almond skin darkened as a silhouette in the sunlight.

"Your books?"

She pursed her lips, maintaining her smile, but cursing herself inwardly. What is wrong with her around this man?

"I used to think of them as my books when my mother was the librarian."

He looked at her finally, his hard jaw softening at her admission.

"So you lost both of your parents young." It wasn't a question. "That's incredibly tough. I lost my mom as a kid, too."

He didn't say anything else, but she could tell there was more to the story. "I'm sorry to hear that."

She breathed in a gulp of fresh air in relief as they entered the bar, the light instantly shifting from blinding to dim. The heavy scent of alcohol clung to the cool air, and she sniffed in appreciation. The smell of old books and the smell of liquor melded well.

"You bastard!" Jane heard the rough exclamation from the bar. It startled her to hear the swear spoken so loudly in the building she was once often shushed in. Whipping around, she identified the yeller just in time to see him collide with Cundo. She stiffened in preparation for a fight, but the two men merely slapped each other on the back and rocked away from each other to greet one another with cheeky grins.

The strange man turned for a moment to size Jane up, his gaze lingering on the satin ribbon in her hair for a moment. His grin widened.

. . .

Til glanced at Jane, then back at Cundo with a conspiratorial twinkle in his eye. Cundo groaned inwardly. This girl already seemed like trouble, he didn't need his burdensome bar buddies, one of whom was the bartender, to interfere in their interactions.

Cundo widened his eyes at Til in a silent plea to let Jane be. He smirked and turned back to the rest of their crew.

"Y'all, Cundo brought a new friend!" he hollered, drawing the attention of the entire bar. The two men he directed his unnecessary shouting at abandoned their tasks at the bar. Cundo quickly steered Jane towards the counter to prevent them from leaving their posts, and her body stiffened at the contact when he placed his hand between her shoulders.

"Look at this, a woman who's not gagging at the touch of your monster paws," quipped Francisco, setting aside the drink he was in the process of making and hopping over the bar to the surprise of a startled Jane, who jerked back.

Cundo grunted in response, and made introductions, solely for Jane's benefit.

"Jane, this is Frank, my bartender, Til, a buddy of mine, and Diego...an old work friend."

"Who ya callin' old?" the third man at the bar jibed, shooting a crooked grin at Jane. Cundo watched her face, waiting for the usual swoon-like reaction to the smile Diego reserved for beautiful women. Her face remained plastered with that calculated, black-and-white movie smile and the dimples that framed it, but did not waver, despite the obvious appreciation in the men's gazes. He wondered if she was simply that used to be ogled.

"It's a pleasure to meet you. Cundo was just escorting me in to socialize." He might've caught the bitterness at the end of the word "escorting" had he not become completely enraptured with the way she said his name. Her tongue seemed to caress the "s" sound before releasing it. For a moment, he thought he'd really like to hear her say every word in the English language just to see what else her voice was capable of.

"Hang out with us tonight," Diego interjected in what would've been a leer had it not come from his stupidly handsome mug.

"Oh, I don't know..." she mused, the boys instantly chiming in to persuade her to stay, though the mischievous dimple she sported told Cundo that she had plans to do so anyway.

Followed by a delighted cheer from his friends, Jane agreed to sit with the group of men, who gathered at the more isolated end of the bar and emptied cups as more people filed in. Cundo greeted the regulars and brought them their usuals before they had the chance to order, while his one waiter and sole busboy circulated, keeping the tables clear, cups full, and books on the correct shelves. Customers brought in crumpled cash in their pockets and desert dust on their boots. Jane, for her part, looked somewhat intrigued by the ebb and flow of the restaurant, and the comfortable relationship he had with his patrons. He got the feeling that she wasn't used to easy banter or casual conversation. Every syllable that came from her mouth appeared strained, like she needed to force herself to talk to people. If she hated socializing so much, why did she seem so eager to join them?

"So Jane, what have you been up to since you graduated high school?" Frank asked. "You went to school with my sister, Melanie, right? Before you left town?"

"Yeah, yeah I did," Jane said, suddenly taking a pull from the straw of her previously untouched daiquiri. Cundo noticed that she dodged the first question, but he wasn't buzzed, nor was he ignorant.

"Well?" he asked, looking at her with enough focus in his eyes that he knew she could tell what he was asking. She looked back, and for the first time, he noticed that her eyes were hazel. The irises looked like a sky full of moving, tumbling clouds.

"I've been working as a counselor for victims of domestic abuse," she responded, her gaze unwavering, and by God, that was the absolute last thing he expected her to say.

"Wow! That must've been rough," Diego murmured sympathetically.

"Are you going to try to pick up a job around here?" Frank asked, immediately tapping into his networking skills. "Because I know some people on the school board. They'd be happy to have you as a counselor at one of the schools." It would've sounded impressive to any other girl, but as a townie, Jane probably knew that everyone knew the people on the school board.

"Oh, how sweet of you," she cooed. "I might take you up on your offer, but I'm all set with what my daddy left behind for right now. I didn't use any of my inheritance after I turned eighteen, and I'm thinking I deserve a bit of a break." She smiled at that last part, and beneath the dimples and artfully tilted head, he saw a weariness that wasn't there before.

"What are you going to do during your 'break'?" Cundo asked, all but using air quotes. Diego shot him a look from his seat on the other side of Jane, probably wondering why he wasn't speaking more kindly to this delicate, sugar-spun creature that for some reason wanted to spend time in his bar.

"Oh, I don't know," she replied listlessly, with a spark in her eye that told him she knew exactly what her plans were. "I might write a bit. I started a few novels back in college, but you know how work can be. I never got to finish them."

"Ooh, what do you write about?" Til asked, genuine curiosity colouring his tone. Til had a secret that only Cundo and a few close friends knew about—he was deeply in love with the written word. For a moment, Cundo felt an irrational surge of possessiveness, as if he was the only one with a right to connect with her because he was the first to discover her.

Hell, he thought, what am I so concerned about, I'm the one that owns an entire public library.

"Oh, this and that. I was considering writing a biography on behalf of my father. He was such an important part of our community."

The boys collectively took swigs of their drinks, nodding in agreement, but not having the eloquence to express the appropriate sentiments.

"Well, this is the right place to do that," he responded. "A lot of research can be done here."

"My thoughts exactly," she simpered, and as she turned the conversation topic to the men and their lives, distracting them and chatting about inane topics, Cundo watched Jane carefully, her expression analytical, her gaze distracted. Wheels were turning in her head, and despite how long it had been since he'd had to pay attention to someone's every move, or even shown average interest in them, he had a deep desire to know exactly what she was thinking.

By the time the regulars had trickled out and the sun had lowered to a lazy puddle of red on the horizon, the guys were ready to head out. Cundo could tell they were reluctant to leave the company of their new lady friend, as if she might leave town again if they let her out of their sight. Cundo felt that way a bit as well.

"Alright, you fools, it's time to get out of here," he said, waving his keys at them as he closed down the register. Diego lifted an amused eyebrow and hustled his protesting friends out of the door. Jane remained at the bar, watching the others go as she chewed on the staw floating in what was left of her watered-down drink. Suddenly, she let the straw drop from her lips and turned her uncomfortably concentrated gaze on him.

"Why did you let me talk to your friends all night?"

His head shot up from the cabinet of glasses he was restocking below the bar. He fumbled with his thoughts, attempting to say something that wouldn't draw her laser-focused attention any further.

"What do you mean, 'let you'?" he asked, wondering what kind of social life she had before coming back home. For a brief second, that led to an image of young Jane -fourteen at the time of her father's death if his calculations were correct- being taken in by the foster system. She had no friends or family close enough to make her feel comfortable in her new life. He pictured her large, hazel eyes, red and glossy with tears, big, round cheeks streaked and void of dimples.

She interrupted the brutal vision with a shrewd tone.

"You could've pawned me off on some townie eager to talk to the orphan that Allen Fairweather left behind," she paused, thoughtfully lifting the cherry from the bottom of her glass. "But instead, you let me stick around. Play with the boys." The side of her mouth quirked up, and Cundo watched with rapt attention as she placed both candy lips around the red fruit and tugged until the stem came loose. She chewed and swallowed, and Cundo watched her throat work as her lips opened back up.

"Is it because I'm a girl?"

His eyes flickered down to his calloused hands, gripping the lip of the bar. He was suddenly very aware that they were alone, right below his living space.

"No, I just thought you might need a friend," he mumbled, looking anywhere other than her piercing gaze. "I figured you might not have a lot of connections in town since you've been gone so long."

Jane watched him before replying, her expression deadly still, unblinking. Cundo felt like an animal in a cage being observed by a scientist.

"How sweet of you."

They looked at each other for a few moments more. Cundo was afraid to look away. Jane's rainstorm-eyes inhaled him, and as he watched them change and her expression remain static, he began to fear that he might get swept away before he could figure her out.

CHAPTER 3

Alligator Gar, Atractosteus spatula

A cacophony of metallic pops echoed about the low range of cliffs beyond the property. The residual sound was like a plane flying by, and Jane tipped back her face and let the wind carry it over her skin. She placed her Glock .40 on the old, leaning picnic table beside her, and fisted her hands at her hips, looking out.

The land her mother had been left was prefaced by her parents' little cabin off the gravel road, and the rest of it stretched out beyond the dry, opaque "lake" beside it. It was really a large, man-made tank, but Jane had thought of it as a lake ever since she was a little girl. Every inch of the land before her looked uninhabited, but only a fool would believe such a thing. From the time she could walk, Jane had toddled along the cracked planes of claypan soil, eventually learning to gravitate towards the beargrass and yucca plants and collect it for her mother, who would weave them into beautiful baskets and fishing creels for the lake. She could still smell the fibers soaking in metal pans in the shed, the water glowing rich reds, pinks, and purples from the cochineal dyes. Those days were the simplest, when she was young enough that her lessons consisted entirely of identifying edible plants and learning how to make fires in the crisp, merciless desert nights. Her mother taught her well, but when she passed, Jane's lessons were cut short, and Detective Fairweather became more determined than ever to make a warrior out of his daughter.

The warrior now stood stock still in the twilight, her only motion the flyaways sticking out of her braid and the fluttering of her loose, linen shirt. She peered out at the makeshift paper target standing at thirty yards, not yet picking up her binoculars to check her marks. She knew her aim was off, but she wasn't concerned- new environments and the heavy night wind played a role in her accuracy, and she practiced often enough that a small change was nothing to be concerned about...yet she wondered.

She'd come out to her father's old home-made shooting range to remind herself of why she was in Fort Zemsta to begin with. For some reason, her trip into town had muddled her brain and confused her. Not as many of the residents remembered her, or were where they had been last. She knew that times had changed, but she wasn't expecting her former home town to be so oddly welcoming...the last thing she remembered from this place was her father's brutal murder and her subsequent abandonment. That could have something to do with it.

That, and the disturbing new development in her mother's old library- Mr. Facundo del Sur.

Jane had discovered more about his identity after lulling his friends into a knowledgeable masculinity that had them telling her everything. Facundo was a Marine vet that had chosen to live in a town full of outlaws, serving them beer alongside law enforcement instead of living out the rest of his days in an untroubled suburb somewhere with a wife and kids.

Another unusual thing about Jane was that she noticed everything that others did not, and none of the things that others noticed first. Facundo's loyal friends had immediately tested what Jane had thought about Facundo's face...

"His face?" she'd asked laughingly. "You want to know if I think he is handsome?"

And the men had looked at her quizzically.

Facundo's scar was apparently garish- it ran from his hairline through his right eye -marring the pupil and the color of the iris- and touched down at his top lip, bringing the corner up in a cruel snarl. The skin was discolored surrounding the scar, as though perpetually dry.

Jane had been able to honestly answer that she did not have any particular opinions about his face.

The first thing Jane noticed about people were their hands. Hands could reveal what type of predator a person was. The older the victim, the rougher the hands of the predator, the younger the victim, the softer and sweatier. Older, bigger victims required work and planning, which required a steady hand and resulted in sores and cuts. Sometimes, depending on how new a person was to their predation, their hands would twitch when they felt their urges, as if their lack of self-control was so close to the surface that they could hardly help but reveal it. Some were odd, mottled, with dirt under the nails. Some were manicured and groomed to perfection.

Facundo's hands were the first thing she looked at. Long, tanned fingers. Callouses, dry but not flaking. Yes, she'd seen his scars, but why would she look at something he'd probably received after one single incident when she could watch his hands- the part of him that had changed with his constant, everyday activities over a matter of years. Stable, constant movements, graceful even. Blunted nails, and a permanently rough index finger.

Trigger finger.

Something about Facundo had made Jane feel something close to trust when she looked at him, and his face had been so secondary to that startling feeling that she hardly paid any attention to the mottled, discolored skin that interrupted his lean, angular features.

She'd rolled her eyes at his friends.

"Out of all the questions you could ask me," she'd chastised. "You ask me something that you can simply observe in my reactions."

"It's just that we're a little protective," Diego had responded to her, watching her carefully. "He's been ostracized in plenty of places because he doesn't...look like everyone else."

Non-violent harm was not something Jane had paid much attention to in her cross-state Justice Killing Road Trip for the past few years. Her focus had always been on those that preyed on the weak, but she hadn't thought of the invisible kind of preying- hurting someone with words.

Something flared in her when she'd heard that, something like protectiveness. Despite the fact that Cundo was at least six feet and four inches tall and he looked like he'd killed at least a dozen people in his prime, she felt a prickling of anger at the thought of someone making him feel less-than because of his face.

It was similar to the bias she'd always received as a young woman.

She was supposed to be so many things as a twenty-four-year-old woman:

- Ignorant of financial matters
- Hysterical when her emotions got the better of her (which would of course be all the time)

- Irrational in the face of a multi-step problem-solution situation
- Quick to fall in love
- Vain, and more concerned with her appearance than with any real-life skills

And the list goes on. Jane was not aware growing up that young women were treated in such a way, and was confronted with all of these stereotypes at once when she went into the foster system. The thought of how she'd been judged the moment someone noticed her gender gave her an inkling of how normal people might immediately judge Cundo and his disfigurement. Luckily, Jane was not normal people.

As she made her way along the beaten path between desert brush from the range to her house, burdened with her gun cases and equipment, Jane pondered this. Perhaps there was a place for her within normal dynamics with other people, it simply wasn't with other normal people. Perhaps she was simply needed by people like her- outsiders. Those who lived outside the bounds of societal normalities.

Something had made Jane forget that Zemsta was a magnet for outsiders, but she was remembering once more. This town had once been a safe place for her, and it may be safe for her again. She just had one more scene to make...

Jane arrived at her shed and scraped the clumps of clay from her boots by the door. The shed looked unassuming from the outside, but it was highly insulated and reinforced with steel beams from the inside. It locked from both the outside and the inside, neither lock able to turn without the combination that she possessed and a set of two keys. Her father had been paranoid about their privacy when she was a child, often hiding things in odd places. As he got older and Jane matured, his fear manifested in different ways, one of which being this shed. Jane relived his fears, replacing the locks on the shed that had been removed by new owners.

Her guns stayed in her house, but she kept her targets in the shed. The papers revealed her marksmanship, something that would be difficult to explain to visitors should they be discovered. Her cover was not maintained by being careless with the details.

A small generator ran the portable air conditioner in the shed, providing the space with enough cool air to make up for the lack of windows and thick walls. This space was where her first sins were committed, in thought rather than action. The day after her father had died, and she realized that the grief, or at least shock, that she'd been expected to feel had been replaced with a hollowness that throbbed in her belly. That hollowness felt an awful lot like hunger.

Hunger for what, she was not sure.

• • •

Facundo scrubbed his hands free of the lingering smell of spilt whiskey, splashing water on his face to wash away some of the fuzziness. The cold dripped down his face, but his skin was too numb to feel wet. The anniversary was coming up, and he knew after years of experience that the anxiety that came with it was unavoidable, outside of his control, unlike everything else.

Semper fidelis.

He looked at the Latin tattoo on the inside of his arm. It was on his right, where the scars became truly mottled. His raw, hairless right arm led to rivers of shiny, pink and brown slashes over his right shoulder, and down his back. One led down his tailbone, another two leading to raw, pocked skin over his thigh. The only scar revealed by his conservative clothing was the one on his face- the one that made people go pale.

Semper fidelis.

The reason why he was a disfigured hermit buying old libraries, he thought viciously. The reason why he couldn't let his past go and simply move on to the colonial-house-with-a-golden-retriever life that he'd been urged to. For years, his job had been to hold himself away from the pleasures of civility, to live on the edge of conflict and crisis, and now he was supposed to forget all that he knew and live by completely different laws. Be flawed in ways he was not and whole in ways that he yet again was not. The Marine Corps had eaten up his youth and aged him quickly. His pride in his country had emerged post-contract, and the escape he'd once found in the service now clung to him and made him a gypsy in his once comfortable homeland.

The West had borne he and his mother into acceptance, something they may not have experienced elsewhere when he was a child. A young, unwed Native American woman with an infant that looked half like her, half like someone else, stumbling into the safety of a place that held her family's history- she'd had dreams beyond an unplanned pregnancy, but she never would have said anything of the sort to her son. She'd been brave, taking him back where she was not sure she'd be wanted, but she knew that it would be the safest place for him out of the entire, unforgiving world. His grandparents had loved him distantly until they passed, and his mother was doting until the end, teaching him everything he would need to know once she was gone.

And she was gone much too quickly.

"Fucker!" someone shouted from outside the bathroom door. Cundo started from his reverie and almost laughed at the vision he made in the mirror- the wide-eyed surprise of a guilty child combined with the garish scars pulling at his features.

"AY," he heard outside the door. "We need to go home and you're the most sober one."

Cundo sighed and retreated from the safety of solitude.

"There he iiiissss," drawled Til, weaving as grabbed Cundo's arm and weaved back to the bar. "We started shelebrating even more after you walked out, you mished it."

"I wasn't aware we were celebrating before," he replied, humoring his friend's inebriated imagination.

"We were shelebrating life!" Til exclaimed, gesticulating towards Frank, who had emptied a bottle of bourbon, looking normal-sized in his large hands, into his gullet as Cundo approached.

"Well that's coming out of your paycheck."

Frank gave a self-satisfied grin.

"Here," Diego offered along with his keys, sliding off his stool. "Use mine and get us home." Diego, though the slightest of them, was the hardiest drinker. He rarely lost his senses, and didn't reveal it much when he did. A hazy look in his eyes and a strained crease in his forehead were the only clues.

Cundo took the keys and ushered the drunk men into the parking lot and felt as if he were herding large, confused toddlers. The men laughed as they fumbled into the sleek truck that Diego kept pretty despite the desert dust. The night had set in, chilling the air enough that the men's drunkenness could potentially leave them ill if he didn't get them home and warm soon enough.

"Have you run into that girl again?" Diego asked from his languor in the passenger seat.

"What girl?" Cundo feigned distractedness, his eyes on the road ahead. The gravel road was gently lit by starlight, and he observed it, grateful that he lived somewhere free of light pollution.

Diego snorted. "So it's going to be like that now? First time a hot girl comes into town and you're going to ignore her?"

"I think that's for the best."

"Well she definitely didn't ignore you."

"What's that supposed to mean?" Cundo snapped, the thought that Jane might have said something about his scars to his friends flashing quickly to the front of his mind. It was irrational, but it was forever and always his very first fear.

"It means that she seems interested," Diego replied without sounding eager to placate. Cundo liked that about him, the fact that he didn't jump when Cundo moved suddenly or immediately attempt to console him when he seemed out of sorts. He wasn't afraid, and their brotherhood had strengthened even after they both retired from service.

Cundo grunted in response, not sure of how to proceed with the line of thought that brought him down. He hadn't had a woman show interest in him for a while, though that was more likely due to his reclusive nature than the face he left the service with. Even with that logic on his side, it didn't keep him from fearing the worst from the opposite sex.

"She's different," Diego said cryptically, as if reading his friend's mind. "I can tell."

Cundo could tell, too, especially later in the evening when he caught her on her bicycle, zipping down the dirt road in the dead of night.

After dropping the men off to their respective homes, the roads were completely empty, which wasn't much of a feat for Zemsta. He'd nearly missed the glint of his headlights bouncing off of the gleaming metal of the bike. It looked old- no, not old. Vintage.

Cundo's breath caught as he took her in, his truck slowing as he involuntarily slipped his foot from the gas pedal. Her head turned in unison with his, their vehicles traveling the opposite direction from one another. The hairs that had come loose from her braid flickered in her speed, and her eyes widened, the beams from his headlights sinking into her thunderous irises.

Her trek did not waver, but she followed him with her gaze, and Cundo watched her in his rearview mirror, watching as she turned back to face the night and pedal faster.

Later on, when Cundo was settling in for the evening, his lamp turned off, his sheets warming around his body, he would think back on that moment and wonder-

Why was she dressed all in black?

CHAPTER 4

Spectral Bat, Vampyrum spectrum

The wind howled, hurling dust and dirt from the ground into the eyes of the marines. "Move!" shouted Facundo, tugging his keffiyeh back up around his mouth. He needed his men to get back to the armament carriers before the storm caught up with them. The dust-laden wind was one thing, but the phosphorescent harbinger that flashed among the clouds behind them was a much greater threat.

Cundo peered up at the clouds and suddenly felt as if he could not run as fast as everyone else. The land stretched out before him, becoming very uneven, and his men ran ahead, seeming to sprint at an inhuman pace, becoming small in the distance. He began to pant, and tried to open his mouth to call out to them to wait, but his throat swelled and the only sound he could emit was a pathetic croak, inaudible over the roaring wind. His skin grew hot and moist under his clothes, and he felt the ground beneath him shudder and begin to swallow him. Cundo's booted feet disappeared into the sand, and as he tried to pull away and walk, everything around him faded, the sand beneath him becoming something else that pulled him down.

His hoarse screams turned into pleads to be released as the force pulling him solidified into two strong hands, wrapped around his ankles. The hands were relentless, and as he struggled, they grew stronger, wider, thicker.

"Help!" his weak voice cried. "Help me!" He realized that he was screaming at the being holding on to his ankles, for now, his body was not being dragged downwards, but being held in place on the edge of a crumbling cliff of some kind.

The scenery around him materialized, and he deduced that he was not on a cliff, but a roof that was slowly falling apart as the tiles slipped from the edge and fell into the abyss below. The hands held him fast to the sloping roof, but the rest of his body was becoming heavy, his keffiyeh whipped from his head and shoulders by the gusts of wind. He felt himself tipping forward. It was too much, he felt, too much effort to keep his body from careening over the edge of the building. He suddenly recognized that it didn't matter whether or not he fell, for he somehow knew that the hands around his ankles belonged to something that would kill him if he remained there anyway.

He leant forward, determined to speed up the process of his dissolution. The wind around him seemed to be sucked under the lip of the roof, and the hands around his ankles were replaced with cold air. He succumbed to gravity, but was surprised when the angle of his descent changed, and his body sailed into the open window of the building that resided just below the roof. How had he not noticed the window before? It didn't matter.

When he landed upright in the center of the room, the wind came to a complete halt, as still as the atmosphere of outer space. Distantly, he recognized the room as a part of the home that he had lived in with his mother, though his mind could not recall a home beyond this one. A sick feeling crept into his arms and legs, seeping into his guts. Something was wrong. He had to go into the hall.

The hallway was dark, but his mind lit the space with a green light. It was wrong, there were no pictures on the walls. Why weren't there any pictures anymore? Why was the carpet growing up from the floor in such an unusual way?

"I can't…"

He heard the muffled cry.

"I can't be with this, I can't have my son around this," the familiar but warped, weak voice wailed.

"You're wrong, something is wrong with you!"

"You don't know what the hell you're talking about," shot back a second voice, mottled and grumbling, like a repulsive beast that could only be heard and horrific to behold.

Cundo ran, but he didn't know what direction he was moving in, and his feet would not carry him properly.

"Sto-" the weak voice choked out the beginning of a protest, but it was cut off. Cundo pumped his feet harder, knowing that he would not make it in time.

He reached a door that hadn't been there before, and it opened without him turning the knob.

A great, hulking beast with strings of white hair upon a poxed, raw scalp stood in the center of the empty room, the edges of Cundo's vision blurry in such a way that the scene before him was the only thing permitted in his sight. The beast hunched over a wisp of a woman who's long, black hair fell beneath her upturned head, quivering with the force of her movement.

That shake, the glossy strands trembling, captured his vision, becoming more solid than anything else that had occured, as though it were straight from a memory, and not his imagination.

The woman was being shaken like a doll by the neck, the beast's puffy, moist hands wrapped fully around her. Her face appeared cartoonish, the delicate features bloated and bruised purple. Her dark eyes bulged from their sockets, and they flickered towards him, widening even further, growing larger and turning from obsidian to a violent swirl of color. Having been discovered, Cundo jerked back, his body beginning to set itself aflame, each molecule being ripped apart. The vision of the dark-haired woman before him began to fade, and the last of her, a bracelet woven with white beads, slipped from her wrist to the floor. Her body vaporized, her particles caught up in the sudden wind that returned through the open window. Dust poured in, his troop's desert filling the room. The beast clasped his hands around nothing as the woman disappeared entirely, and having nothing to occupy his abominable gaze, he turned his attention to Cundo, who suddenly felt smaller, weaker. Looking down, he saw that his arms had become frail. The arms of a teenager, a boy not yet prepared to defeat the animal in front of him.

The beast laved his wide, dripping tongue over chapped lips, and just as he was about to move towards Cundo, the dust that had begun occupying the room swelled like a wave, overcoming everything in sight.

Cundo braced himself against the door, not willing to create more distance between himself and the monster, not wanting to be swept away, never to take vengeance…

The wall rose, and the room became a roaring sea of sand, moving to the whim of the stormy wind, a cobra dancing to the tune of a flute, prepared to strike. Cundo stood against the storm and waited for the impact-

A gasp.

Cundo dragged air into his lungs, struggling to sit up from his suffocating, horizontal position. He opened his eyes wide, and at first he saw nothing, but as his vision cleared, he realized that he was not standing-off against a desert storm, but caught up in his bedsheets, sweat-soaked and panting. The air around him was stiflingly still, and despite his body and his rapid pulse's protests, he swung out of bed and escaped his room, stumbling to the terrace of his loft, allowing the cold metal of the railing to cut through his heated skin and wake him.

He slowly tipped his head back and forth, as if he could fling the dream from his mind. With the dreams that plagued every minute of his sleep came a sick feeling- a feeling of wrongness, as though his mind wanted him to be aware of the wrongs that surrounded him even in the moments that he was supposed to feel peace. It was like the feeling he'd had after his accident in the service...it had been months of recovery. Skin grafts and surgeries to repair internal damage accompanied by restless, forced bed-rest in which the surface of his skin either felt unbearably itchy, or on fire. The wrong-feeling plagued him from that incident forth, sinking from his skin into his bones, where he would feel wrong every night after.

The explosion of one of their artillery vehicles had been accidental, it turned out. It was frustrating to know that he'd been unmanned by a mere accident and not an act of deliberate violence. Instead, he was thrown into the air, nearly blown to pieces, just touching the skirts of the explosion and still suffering eternally for it...all because of an accident. It wasn't like his mother's death.

Her death had been buried thoroughly when he left for the service. It was not until the PTSS settled in that the memories came roiling back to upend his already tumultuous life. His therapist said that trauma worked like that- balled up together like bile in a gallbladder and turned into one, hard, painful stone.

Cundo ran his shaky hands over the scars on the right side of his face. He returned, reluctantly to his bedroom, and crossed to the bare, mesquite dresser that dominated the opposite wall of his room, The only objects gracing its surface were a worn leather box, a stack of miscellaneous books he'd liberated from the library below, and an iron vase that had been intended to add a decorated look, but only served to emphasize the minimalist aesthetic that he always seemed to create.

The leather box was difficult to open, the wood below the material having been warped with water damage and age. When he pried it open, he moved a few of the faded pictures aside, a couple scraps of fabric and braids of baby hair. Beneath it all was the object that he could not bear to part with. The object that he would opt to save first in the event of a fire.

A woven bracelet with white beads.

• • •

Miles away, and several turns off the county-tended roads, Jane tossed and turned in her own bed. Her body seeped with ice-cold sweat, and her dreams dripped with even colder images.

The event replayed every few seconds like a glitching internet video. Jane's body would move without her feet carrying her, getting closer to the living room, and then it would cut off. Over and over. Closer...and back. Closer...and back. She urged herself to move in and stay, stay to watch, but she wasn't sure that she was ready. Her body itched with the need to see what was happening, even though in the back of her mind, she was sure that she already knew.

Murmuring voices pricked at her ears, and she listened to the urgent tones, the sound waves pulling her closer to the scene.

"Listen, I don't know what position you're in-"

"Stop trying to talk to me, there's no use."

The voices were stark against the haziness of the dream.

"There's no reason to do things this way. Trust me, it only gets worse from here if you go through with it."

"You don't know what you're talking about."

"You're right, tell me what's going on, tell me what you need."

Jane's vision suddenly widened and included the full scope of the living room. Two men stood in the center, one in pajama pants, the other in black-clothes too warm for the desert, even at night. He held a gun.

"Just talk to me," whispered the pajama-clad gentleman gently, as if speaking to an anxious child, and not an armed home invader.

"I don't need to talk," the unwanted visitor replied nervously, his grip on his gun tightening. Jane felt the need to do something, but she knew that her presence would disrupt things in a very unwelcome way.

"Please...I know you're not a killer," he continued tenderly. "I've seen your record, you're not a violent man. Do not become one."

The bearer of the weapon clamped his mouth shut firmly. He did not seem to change his mind, yet he was not firing. The other man stood stock-still and seemingly at peace. He was not upset at the barrel facing him.

It was in that moment that Jane felt her body once more. She moved without wanting to. Her throat emitted a choked gasp at the scene, as if seeing it for the first time.

The armed man's gaze jerked to where she hid. The other man was suddenly not at peace, and reached for the bookshelf to his right. Jane knew somehow that a gun was placed there.

And then there was a shot.

The man's pajamas turned red from the waistband to the ankles, and the rest of his body seemed to turn red, too. Not red, but brown. No, not brown, purple. He went rigid and crumpled to the floor like a rag doll, and none of the visions before her seemed real. His body turned waxen before her, the brilliant red no longer the color of his skin and clothes, but just a glistening trickle from his abdomen that solidified into a filmy matte upon the rest of the figure on the floor.

Jane looked up, unwilling to leave the figure behind, but knowing that the intruder meant her harm. The expression that she saw on his face was a surprise to her, for he looked as shocked as she did that he'd committed the act. Jane braced herself to run, but her body betrayed her and refused to move an inch. The man didn't bother to raise his gun to her, though she was but a mere slip of a girl, unarmed.

Not for long.

She leapt towards the bookcase and seized the Glock she'd held many times before in her slight hands. The man did not react to the sight of the firearm except to look even more contrite.

"I'm sorry," his voice trembled. Her chest heaved, and she began to struggle to breathe.

His gun remained at his side, and to her horror, streaks of remorse erupted from his eyes and trickled down his face. The image of the man seemed to expand and then suddenly was sucked out of the door. The door opened and closed like a prop on a stage, swallowing the man behind it, and Jane felt the Glock disappear from her hands. Looking down, the waxen figure began to melt into the carpet and turn everything the color that belonged only inside a person.

The carpet grew hard with the wax and turned into wood, and her face rushed towards it, her nose turning at a sickening angle against the flat of the floor. Something (an elbow, she seemed to know) pressed into the back of her head and made the pain worse. Her arms twisted in a very wrong way behind her back, and as she became aware of her lower half, she grew cold.

A sweaty hand held her wrists, and legs much bigger than her's pushed her knees apart. Something bad was about to happen, and she was old enough to know what it was, but young enough that she had never prepared herself for it, even though her father had tried.

She knew what was coming, knew what was happening, knew when it was over. She was alone, and no one was coming to get her, because the figure that was her father had turned to wax on the floor and melted, and that was the only thing holding up the bubble that had once surrounded her and kept Bad Things at bay.

Well, the Bad Things were here. And they could not be stopped.

She felt hot fluid trickling from her in a way it never had before. Oddly, she felt relieved that the blood was there, as if it confirmed that what was happening to her was unwanted, unwelcome...wrong. Her body shed syrupy, staining tears for her abuse, and in the darkness, there on the hardwood floor, her blood spilled out of her and began to flood the room, not stopping to solidify like wax.

It was moving and alive, and it crept up the walls to fill it from top to bottom, and the man above her was washed away on a wave of red. Jane rolled over into the pool around her, lifting her body as it rose, luxuriating -now that the spectre behind her was gone- in the comforting, warm wetness that proved she still lived, and was not a frozen, wax figurine.

The blood filled every inch of the room, and she sensed that it was no longer her own. It fed her, and she grew so large that she herself filled the room like Alice eating cake.

She giggled mirthlessly and fell beneath the surface of the raging sea of blood.

"More!" she cried out, somehow able to speak without air.

"More!"

The fluid bubbled and rose.

"More."

She began to sob.

"More…"

It was her blood now. Wherever it was coming from, it came from her, too.

"More," she gurgled, and was no longer able to breathe.

Jane arched off her mattress with the deepest, most painful breath she'd ever taken. Her chest ached with the force of it, and she grasped at the ribbon that closed her nightgown at her breastbone. Loosening it accomplished nothing.

Springing from her bed and ignoring the pins and needles that bit at her legs left uncirculated by tangled sheets, she stalked out of her stifling bedroom and out of the cabin entirely.

The open, unending desert landscape outside of her bedroom had always freed her as a child. She gulped in night air, relishing the feel of it tickling her bare body standing under the sky. It weighed on her like a blanket, and she held it up with her naked shoulders as she prowled into the darkness, her feet moving in the familiar direction of the shed with only the light of the stars illuminating her way. The rocks stabbed at her bare feet, reminding her that humans were too soft to live like animals in the desert. She refused to flinch, pressing her calloused soles into the earth to remind her that she was more animal than human. The shed was colder in the night, but she couldn't feel anything the way she was trembling with focus. She searched among the boxes that had yet to be unpacked, tearing out the bare minimum of what she needed, uncapping bottles and dipping brushes before she'd even had time to choose a canvas. She could not leave her thoughts unformed lest they overwhelm her and take over her senses. She'd felt this way before, usually after a nightmare, but this was different. She was here now.

Dragging the body-sized canvas into the dirt outside, she began slashing paint across its surface, paying no mind to what paint she used, as the moon deprived everything of color. She threw across the white space the image of the man in her living room, the whites of his eyes exaggeratedly widened, the visage of an immortally haunted man. She eventually gave up on the brushes and used pallet knives to scrape the paint into submission. Her hands grew dark with the paint, the skin cool and taut as it dried in the midnight breeze, covered and recovered with more layers of excess paint. She grew desperate, her shaking hands dropping the pallet knives and resorting to using her nails and the pads of her fingers to create the image of the man who killed her father.

Something vicious in her wanted to memorialize the moment that made him human. She wanted to create a punishment that existed away from him, unknown, a version of him that despite whatever reward he received for his deeds lived on to remember a moment that made him weak. Vulnerable.

Almost as vulnerable as a fourteen-year-old girl watching her father, best friend, and entire world get shot.

As her hands became unrecognizable, she developed the sudden, urgent notion that she needed to return to the bath of blood she'd dreamt. Her hands flew to her throat and slid up and down, coating her face, chest, shoulders, and arms with what felt like the congealing blood of her prey. It grew colder until the drying substance pilled and chafed against her skin, and in her frustration, she fell to her knees and threw her arms out.

Her body bowed backwards, the opposite of worship, the foil to humility, and as her head tipped to the sky, her jaw fell open and she let out a bone-chilling scream.

I cannot be a victim if I am a predator.

She could not be a victim if she was a predator.

Her shriek could certainly be heard across the desert. The cracked earth must've inhaled her cries and breathed them back into the open sky, because she could hear it echo back to her over the mountains in the distance. She let out another yell, not allowing the mask she formed for Zemsta to muffle her distress into a girlish scream, the kind that pierced the ears but sounded like a damsel in a black and white movie instead of an animal lost in the wilderness. She refused to stifle her roar in her desert, under her stars. Her feet grew roots into the ground and she kneeled solidly, not in submission but in signification that this was her land. Her dust. Her canvas. Her memories. Her pain.

She could almost feel the blood on her hands as she hollered into the sky her wordless vow of vengeance, the promise that she would never forget the moments that turned her into this creature. She would never let go. She would never be normal again. She would never submit again. She would never be a victim again.

In the distance, thunder rumbled.

CHAPTER 5

Tigerfish, Hydrocynus vittatus

"Love came to me..."

Her truck came to a rumbling stop.

"I feel so gooooood..."

She took a steadying breath, not for her nerves, but for her cover.

"Oh lo-uve came to me-"

She rolled up her cardigan sleeves into charming folds, feeling like a roast pig in the heat.

"And knock, knock, knock on woo-" She turned the car off and leapt out into the sun, searching for the vehicle that she already knew she wouldn't see. It had been too long, he would have gotten a new one.

The diner, to her disbelief, was still in business, the sign unchanged except for a paint job that had probably been new about five years ago. This town had once felt like a collective family member that had abandoned her to the abuse she suffered in foster care, but she still found a nostalgic charm in certain things. For example, this diner was the location of many after school sundaes and french fries (probably too many) and a place that she and her father had shared. They used to laugh at the fact that one half of the building was dedicated to the dive diner, which sold locally-made cajeta and honeycomb candies. The other half was a tire shop.

Dust particles drifted in the still air of the diner, the clinking of dishes and smell of migas startling the senses that had become accustomed to the silence and sterility of her empty cabin for the past few days. The sudden sensory assault brought on a rush of memories, and it almost overwhelmed her. Then she saw him.

He had hunched a bit with age, and the laugh lines around his eyes had deepened. Other than that, it was clear that time was no match for the good humor of her father's old friend. His head rose.

"Janie," he said simply, a smile revealing the slightly crooked teeth of someone born before the readiness of orthodontics.

"Officer Lasica," she grinned back, her tongue not touching her alveolus on the "l" in the typical fashion of Polish names. She'd said his name many times as a child, but saying it as an adult felt different. She wasn't sure why.

His familiar good humor radiated from him, and he rose to pull her into a tight embrace. Every single one of her nerve endings lit aflame, and she fought her natural urge to thrust the man away from her. He patted her on the back roughly, as if she were a beloved nephew.

"It's good to see you, pretty girl, I've missed you so much. Look at how big you are!"

She'd heard sentiments such as these in the past few days, but it was a new concept to her. No one had ever thought she'd "gotten so big" in foster care because no one had ever known her for long. And "getting big" as a foster kid was a terrible thing- it meant you were getting closer to being eternally bereft of a family.

"That's not what a young lady wants to hear," she replied jokingly, and he let out a full-bellied laugh, jarring memories of watching this man laugh with her father to the forefront of her mind.

"Just as sharp as your daddy," he chuckled. "He'd be so proud of you." She wrinkled her nose at that. How would he know? He had no idea what kind of person she was. She doubted that her father would be proud of the fact that she'd become the kind of creature that he'd hunted in his days on the force.

"So beautiful!" he let out, good-naturedly. She gave a tight smile. Her supposed beauty was merely a skin that could be shed.

"It's good to see you again," she changed the subject. "I feel like a stranger here, yet everyone remembers me."

"You'll never be a stranger here, pretty girl, no matter how long you've been away."

She smiled politely and pushed down the rare and uncharacteristic sickness that hadn't plagued her during deception since she was green in her craft. It was a useless feeling.

"So, about what I called you for," she said directly, trying not to sound impatient. Lasica gave an amused grin, as if her serious matter were nothing more than a child playing dress-up.

"Yes, I dug up some of the old things I had on your dad's case," he pulled out an old accordian folder and pulled out a stack of mismatched papers. He licked a finger and exhaled, settling in to sift through the papers the way old men do. Jane kept her hands under the table to prevent them from revealing how eager she was to get a hold of the information.

"There's another couple boxes, but I didn't think you wanted to see them," he said cryptically. From across the sticky diner table, she could see that clipped to some of the forms were images of the crime scene, body, and bullet wound. Even random pictures from around her home, eerily familiar, yet somehow unlike the rooms she lived in now. If he had such pictures in this folder, what was so unnerving in the boxes he had that she could not see?

"You see, Janie," he said on a sigh, avoiding her eyes completely. "We found some things that you might not like. And I've done everything I can to keep this out of the media...you have no idea what would happen if people found out."

"What are you talking about?" Jane asked tremulously, her heart beating hot in her ears.

"Your daddy was a good man."

"What are you talking about," she repeated, no longer asking, but demanding.

"He..." Lasica looked down at the papers again, as if they bore the words he needed to say. "I was very close to your father. He was a good person, I don't think he meant for it to get that far."

Jane waited, hands tucked beneath her thighs, her feet bouncing on the floor beneath her. A waitress slowed by their booth, but passed quickly after catching a glimpse of the gory pictures strewn on the table. He inhaled deeply and continued.

"He was such a good man, I think, that all the work he did on the force twisted him up inside. It was hard to find this out, but...he got into some bad things, Janie. All the information we had on the head of operations through our miles of the border...it was false. He brought in false information."

Of all the facts to shake her, this one was the least expected one.

"That's not true!" she snapped, some of the predatory snarl she reserved for prey biting out on the last syllable. Lasica did not look surprised by her reaction.

"Like I said, I don't think he meant any harm. It's hard raising a child alone...it's more than likely where your inheritance came from-"

"Don't," she interrupted, quiet but deadly. "My father did not take bribes."

"None of us want to think of him that way," he said sadly. "But it looks like that might be the reason he was accosted. Not because of his investigation, but because...well, I guess they were tired of paying him. Maybe they found someone else inside, I don't know. But one thing you can be sure of is that I won't tell a soul. I want to protect his reputation as much as you do."

Jane curled her lip and considered what "reputations" meant to her. They were a cover, a shroud over truth to protect the ignorance and sensibilities of weak men. She invented them at will and used them to kill. Her father had no need of a reputation, for every moment of his life, he had been honorable, and could prove it with each action he took.

"What information do you have? Specifically? I want to know."

"I don't think..." he hesitated.

"I want it." He looked her in the eye.

"Alright. I'll collect some things for you and bring them by when I can," he said, watching her curiously. Perhaps there was something in her tone, the kind of terse demand that she would give to someone she was in the middle of suffocating. She didn't mean to, but something about her father's old friend, a man she had trusted implicitly as a child, was triggering the almost unignorable need to strike him. Crouched, claws extended, like an angry wildcat with her hair on end. The feeling was curious. She had changed a great deal from the innocent girl that had sat here years ago. She felt her father's ghost over her shoulder, urging her.

"Yes, get those to me as soon as you can," she bit out carefully, trying to regain her sweetness, but showing a bit too much tooth.

They spent another etiquette-mandated hour discussing polite things, and he expressed the correct amount of remorse for her difficult teen years. She painted colorful and false images of a girl mature enough to not need a steady set of parental figures traveling the state in one adventure after another.

Lasica was delighted by the tales, enjoying the clearly fabricated joy that she expressed. It was a far preferable experience to having her world turned over by unbelievable accusations against her father. She was comfortable with her lies, and it was a subtle reclamation of her authority. When you build the ground your opponents stand on, you control whether or not they fall.

"Well, I guess I'll see you in mass later, pretty girl," Lasica concluded, throwing down cash on the table despite Jane's gentle, faux protesting.

"Ah, yes." Shit. She'd forgotten the ritual of Sunday evening mass. It was easier for the farmers to go after their morning chores were done. She had gone with her family for years before her life became a twisted carcass of its previous self. Now she supposed she would have to go again. *Let's hope I don't get struck by lightning when I cross the threshold.*

They said their goodbyes, and Jane forced down the acidic feeling in her throat at his proximity. She didn't want to attend mass, nor did she want to attend a gathering of people that had once been her community, but if there was any way to win the good opinion of her small town, it was with her hands clasped together in a pew.

. . .

Ding...

Ding...

The old Polish church blended seamlessly with the landscape around it, small like a chapel, colorful like the Mexican cathedrals that graced the larger border towns. But the people within the church did not blend in quite as well today. Yes, old babcias and abuelas came in with wrinkled, serious faces, and children came in wearing their shiniest suit, but in the front pew, a new mother sat, and a row of large, menacing-looking men sat beside her.

Ding...

Cundo squirmed uncomfortably on the hard, wooden seat. As a large man, he often worried that he was blocking the people behind him if he were unlucky enough to find himself at the front of a crowd. It was unavoidable today, however, and he would take his punishment quietly in deference to the lady of the hour- the tiny bundle sleeping soundly in her mother's arms.

Frank was not only his bartender, but a close friend as well, and the four friends that spent time together at the bar also supported one another during important moments, like this one. Frank gazed lovingly at the top of his petite wife's head, her inky hair matching that of the soft little miracle she held. Baby Isabella's delicate white christening gown reminded Cundo of the frothy confections that Jane often wore when he caught her around town. Looking down at his own, stiff suit, he wondered if he had ever looked so vulnerable, so harmless. Then again, Jane doesn't exactly seem harmless to him, simply the antithesis to his dark, functional choices of attire.

He peered around the church, the old chandelier lights dimmer than the light coming in through the stained glass windows. The families that lined the pews were the purest cores of the community. The outlaws that ran through the town didn't bother coming to church, because everyone knew what they were. Cundo usually sat in the back, worshipping separately in silence during the "old people" masses on Saturday nights. He wasn't one to worship for the sake of deception. He did it for himself and for the sake of his poor mother's restless soul. There was no need to convince anyone that he was a God-fearing Catholic when anyone who saw his face already thought that he was the Devil himself.

It was an interesting thing to ponder on, his own lack of purity, as he sat near the most chastening thing in the world- a baby. Not for the first time he wondered what kind of father he would be. Would he be like Frank, who looked down at the product of his love for his wife like she was the greatest thing to ever have been invented? Or perhaps he would be like Til, who had reacted to Isabella's birth like one would react to receiving a new toy for Christmas. He was thrilled to have the opportunity to be the uncle that did everything her parents wouldn't.

His greatest fear was that he'd be like Diego, who now watched the baby with undisguised horror, wrinkling his nose whenever she whimpered or gave a wail. Diego clearly did not have a desire to be a father, which is perhaps the key ingredient in being a strong paternal figure. Although, Cundo thought, many said that all it would take is one moment in the presence of his own child to change that forever. Perhaps that is what Cundo needed to satiate the emptiness in him...a family.

As his mind swirled with chaotic thoughts of life and purpose, and the church sat still with contradicting peace, his eyes wandered. They rested on a spot of gold that looked wilder than the gilding of the pews. His heart froze and then stuttered back to life, as if forgetting for a moment that it was responsible for keeping him alive. Mierda. It's her.

Jane sat across the aisle and three rows back, boldly sitting between two close families, despite the fact that solitary people often sat in the back, their loneliness hidden in the shadows. Jane did not seem to know she was alone, however, and Cundo found himself wishing that he was sitting beside her, if only to be able to lean in and inhale the air that sat around her head in a golden halo. He wanted to know if it felt as hot as the sun it appeared to be, or if it smelled like a field soaking in light during the summer. That's what she looked like.

Her face was carefully lain with reverence, but he couldn't determine what lay beneath it. Was she secretly terribly bored? Angry? Amused? He wasn't sure why, but he desperately wanted to know the mechanics of Jane's thoughts.

She seemed at peace in her row, her expression the perfect mask of angelic serenity, her sundress modestly layered with some kind of sweater, and her hair braided around her head, as if to show off the length without letting it down and wild. He wanted to see it down and wild.

Just as the impure thoughts were entering his mind, her eyes flicked up to meet his ogling. The intensity of her gaze sent a scorching sensation from somewhere around his belt buckle down to the tips of his toes. He knew that if he tried to get up and move in that moment, he would be unable to. Something like amusement flashed in Jane's molten irises, and her lips quirked up. Just as quickly as she'd looked at him, she looked back down at her hymnal. Cundo whipped back around to face the altar, upon which Father Juan was holding up the eucharist. He felt Diego's eyes on him, and when he turned, his friend was smirking, flicking his eyes back and forth between him and Jane. Cundo rolled his own and ignored him, though the burning feeling had spread up to his face, resting on his scars.

"Bendito seas, Señor, Dios del universo, por este pan, fruto de la tierra y del trabajo del hombre…." Father Juan droned, his deep, unconcerned tone echoing the liturgy of the Eucharist through the arches of the old church. Cundo closed his eyes and tried to get swept away by it.

"…que recibimos de tu generosidad y ahora te presentamos; él será para nosotros pan de vida."

The congregation stood, knelt, and sat reverently, doing as they should. And all the while, Cundo, feeling like a blasphemous heathen, went through the motions with nothing but Jane on his mind. When he should have been praying, he was cursing himself for wanting so badly to turn back around. When the music started up, he strained to hear Jane's voice over the crowd. Would she sing in a girlish soprano, or belt out deep, husky, womanly notes?

The parish began to line up to receive communion, and due to the elongated blessing that Father gave to baby Isabella before serving her mother, the line to his right moved faster. Suddenly, he was standing next to Jane, his shoulder just a hair's breadth away from the crown of her golden head. His breathing quickened.

They bowed in unison before their Eucharistic ministers. As she bowed, she turned her head slightly to lock eyes with him. In one, breathtaking movement, her lips curled up in a wicked smile and she winked at him. All at once, the devilish grin was gone, and she was back, wide-eyed before her minister, hands cupped before her.

Cundo practically sweated as he faced Father Juan, who looked at him disapprovingly before saying, "El Cuerpo de Cristo," and making a cross with the Eucharist with pursed lips.

"Amén," Cundo replied, wondering if it was a sin to resent a parishioner as you served them the Eucharist.

Back in his pew, his line of friends stared holes in him, their heads comically creating a fan as they leaned around one another to see him. They seemed aghast at something, and he felt as if he should know what it was. It wasn't until he stood and saw his reflection in the steel basin of Holy Water nestled to the left of the altar that he realized he was red as a turnip. The entirety of the nosey congregation had probably also noticed the exchange between he and Jane, even if it felt private. Not a single Catholic in the building lacked the borderline magical power of observation that Mexican and Polish families passed down to each generation. He should've known that people would take note.

He felt the heat of shame flutter around his ears as he considered how people saw the situation. They probably conceived the image of a disfigured beast leering down at a tiny local girl who lacked the protection of a family. Even he could understand the perception.

As mass came to a close, and the regular parishioners filed out, leaving Frank and his wife to christen Isabella before their guests, unwelcome thoughts filtered into Cundo's mind through the holes Jane had burnt into him with her focused gaze. It had been years since Cundo had dated a woman the way a normal man could. He had intimate companions from time to time to quench his loneliness, but only when the need was so strong that it drowned out the thought of his mother chastising him for abandoning his faith and becoming a puta. Like any red-blooded man, he needed closeness with another human, but out of spite, he chose loneliness over the signature flinch he witnessed when another person caught sight of his injuries. He'd never forget the first time he was with a woman after his accident, and her horrified expression when he took off his shirt. Even the memory of it was enough to shake him when he was supposed to be beaming with happiness at the new family on the altar.

Diego stood beside him, watching with mild interest and amusement as Isabella began fussing at the water being poured over her head. The priest did everything with deliberate movements, efficient, unconcerned by the screaming infant, but her parents coddled and whispered to her, upset by the delicate snuffles and squeaks of the baby. Cundo watched on in awe. It was a wonder how everyone else in the world could see a little creature such as this and think it beautiful but typical, at best, and that its parents would still be blown away by it each day of its life. He wondered, not for the first time, if he would ever have a chance to experience that.

CHAPTER 6

Saltwater Crocodile, Crocodylus porosus

"Look, look, look!"

"Ssshhhh, she's going to hear you–"

"She's right there, go over there!"

"Stop fucking pointing!"

Cundo slapped Til's hand down, causing Frank to chuckle in that lumberjack way of his.

After Jane's little winking stunt the afternoon before, the boys had been teasing Cundo, and urging him to make a move on Jane. She was clearly trouble, and lightyears out of the league of a disfigured loner with no one left to live for. Nothing on earth could compel him to ask her on a date.

"Shit, I'll do it," drawled Diego, casually taking a swig of his beer.

Except that.

"No," Cundo said, too quickly. "I'll- I'll ask her, I'm just waiting until she picks a book."

Jane had been perusing the aisles of the library half of the bar, ordering nothing but a Shirley Temple and sucking on cherries as she flipped through book after book. It was torture for Cundo, who was gradually wondering more and more what those fair, delicate hands would feel like on his own skin, which was not nearly as smooth as the pages of books.

"That's such a bullshit answer," teased Til, whose typical energy was still present, but diminished by the nights he'd been spending at Frank's, helping with Isabella during late Red Light shifts. Cundo shot a glare at Til.

"She just makes me nervous...doesn't she kind of seem...fake? Like she's not really talking to you, like she's speaking from a script or something?"

The men looked at him as if he'd just leapt onto the bar and began stripping.

"Alright," Diego began, setting his drink down and shifting as if to get up.

"No." Diego looked at him abruptly.

To prevent Diego from swooping in and snatching the petite woman out of her cozy nest of books, Cundo stood and made his way over to her with leaden legs. As her visage grew closer, he became more unsure of how she would react. There was no evidence that she was a heterosexual woman interested in being accosted with requests for a date. Other than her wink, which Cundo believed could be indicative of numerous things, she had not shown any sign that she wanted to spend time with him. They hardly knew each other, for God's sake.

Jane looked up from the worn paperback she was caressing and gave him what to others might look like an easy smile, but to Cundo, looked like the bunching of muscles in a panther's back legs. Just before striking.

"Well hello there, Mr. Facundo, how are you doing this evening?" she asked playfully, marking her page with her thumb and leaning casually against the bookcase. Her demeanor was in complete opposition to his, as he stood rigidly, his weight bouncing between his feet rather than settling on his good leg.

"Hey, I just wanted to see how you liked the bar. You know, with this being your old library and all." Her smile faltered, but she didn't break.

"It's still the library. Just, with alcohol. Which may very well be an improvement," she quipped, the dimple returning. Her joking put Cundo at ease, he felt more like he was talking to a real person rather than an actress in the middle of a scene.

"Do you think you might want to stick around later, after I leave? I let Frank handle the stragglers and lock up," he said gruffly.

"Stick around?"

"Yeah, you know...maybe we can go do something." He hoped that she remembered he lived there and that he didn't sound like a sleazy older man trying to lure her back to his home.

She watched him carefully for a moment. His pulse pounded in his ears, and he wondered what he wished for more- for a chance to get this woman alone and investigate her character, or for her to put him out of his misery and shoot him right there on the spot.

• • •

She wanted to shoot him right there on the spot.

This man's incessant need to pin her with his gaze and acknowledge her everywhere she went, thwarting her attempts to blend into the background and be invisible enough to do her job was driving her up the wall. She had so much to accomplish and little time to do it. Nothing good could come of a 6'5" obstacle drawing attention to her.

She pressed her lips into a thin smile and studied him, weighing the pros and cons of answering in the negative. Men were predictable up to a point, she'd come to understand. They could almost always be anticipated, but rejection was one of those wrenches that threw everything into chaos. Many members of the male species did not take it well, and she'd played victim a number of times before to the bullying of an unsatisfied young man who believed his romantic regard to be an honor of the highest degree. Little did these men know they were dealing with a hunter of men.

But something told Jane that Cundo was not a bully, and the grim resolution in the way he offered his time to her seemed as if he already expected to be let down. Perhaps getting to know him was a ticket into the cogs of the town- he seemed to know everyone.

As soon as she had that thought, she flinched against it, wondering where it had come from. Excuses. At her flinch, Cundo blushed, his steady gaze flickering downward. She wondered at that, but decided that her best course of action from here on out was to stop psychoanalyzing the man and assume as much naivete as possible.

"Sure," she offered hesitantly, trying to relax her jaw. "What do you want to do?"

"Oh…" he looked at his feet, then up at the ceiling, squinting. Jane wondered if he'd considered the possibility of her saying yes. "How about a movie? There's a theatre in town."

Jane was familiar with the small, two-theatre cinema in the larger, neighboring town. She hoped that his unoriginal suggestion was a result of a lack of preparedness.

"Sounds good. Let me know what time." She shot one more tense smile and carried her book over to the lounge of reading chairs, leaving a very uncertain Cundo still facing the bookcase.

Jane gazed into the mirror above her bathroom sink. She and Cundo had thought she ought to go home and let him finish some work in his office while she got ready. She wasn't sure how long normal women took to get ready for a date, as she'd only been on dates with people she intended to divest of their lives. Nevertheless, she put in the amount of effort that she put into her scenes; carefully painted face with wide, cat-eye liner, cherry pink lips, and fair skin with just a bit of blush to them. She donned a light, rose dress that accented the flair of her hips and the swell of breasts that she often tried to mask with A-lined clothing and loose sweaters. She opened one of the unpacked boxes marked "SHOES" in her bedroom and stared at the contents.

She hadn't had much opportunity to indulge in the personal whimsies that interested her outside of her scenes, one of which was her shoe collection. She had functional boots and tennis shoes, dainty ballet flats and sandals, and somewhere in the back of her scene-related assortment, there was a selection of shoes that had called to her in the stores she'd found them in.

She tentatively removed a pair of pink shoes from the box, fondling the poured-on pink pleather and the steel spikes that emerged from the six inch stiletto heel on each one. She pressed the pad of her finger into the tip of one of the spikes, testing its sharpness. By seven pm, she had the pair of spiked, pink heels strapped to her feet as she waited on the living room couch for Cundo. There were too many things attached to the sentiment of wearing her second-favorite shoes for her to analyze it now.

The trout-themed clock on the wall of the living room, a relic leftover from her father's residency, ticked away the time before her. She sat, impatiently shaking her leg against the sofa, watching the faux fishing line that acted as the minute hand move further and further past the twelve. He was sixteen minutes late.

Jane had been late for her fake dates. She often waited in her car, counting the minutes precisely, solely so that she could arrive with a bashful smile and tell her target that it took her longer to get ready than she thought it would. She doubted that Cundo had the same excuse for being late.

It was 6:24 pm by the time her doorbell rang, Cundo's presence preceded by headlights flashing between her window blinds. She found herself taking her time retrieving her purse and moving to the door, not wanting to seem too eager. She checked herself in the mirror hanging above the fireplace right before she placed her hand on the doorknob. The waterfall of copper curls and the filmy, pink dress made quite a vision. It took more effort than she could admit to tamper down the desire to look presentable for the man on the other side of the door. He doesn't matter. He's a means to an end. He's exactly like everyone else.

• • •

Cundo could quite honestly say that the woman who opened the door looked nothing like anyone else he'd ever met. Her flower-petal skin looked completely untouched, as if this was her first time stepping out into the grimy, dirty world. Her dress was yet another thing that looked like something he couldn't touch- too pristine, too good.

Too sweet.

He had to hold his breath in his mouth for a minute before uttering a sound. He was afraid that an unwanted compliment would come bursting out of his mouth.

"I'm sorry I'm late," he said instead. Idiot.

She grinned, dropping her eyelashes just a tad.

"Nothing to worry about, I just finished getting ready."

Instead of replying to what felt like a lie, though he couldn't say why, he simply led her back to his truck and opened the passenger side door.

He'd had to clear junk mail and soda water bottles from the front seat before running a vacuum cleaner over the carpet. He was quite proud of the exterior of his lifted, chrome-gilded, four-door Ford, but the interior gave the distinct impression of a bachelor. Jane lifted her hand delicately when he helped her into the seat, accepting the obvious help she needed considering the fact that the floor of the vehicle arrived at her waist, but he hardly felt her weight as she stepped in. He tried not to notice her legs as they folded into the front seat, nevertheless, his eyes wandered downwards, and he couldn't help but notice the flexing muscles in her calves as she worked to propel herself into the cab of the truck. She must be a runner, he surmised, but his mind took a warmer turn, and he wondered what other kinds of vigorous exercise she might enjoy.

It took all the self-control that Cundo possessed to get in his car and start driving without doing or saying something stupid. As soon as he shut the door, he was enveloped by the scent of vanilla and lavender, like someone was baking cookies in his passenger seat. He permitted himself a glance at the fairy next to him, and quickly looked back at the road when he saw that she was staring at him.

"So, I hope you like scary movies," he said shakily, somehow sounding angry about the statement. She giggled in a deliberate way, sounding far too pleased by the idea of scary movies.

"I love them! But I do get scared easily, so you'll have to tell me when to close my eyes."

Cundo pursed his lips, not answering. This was the kind of demeanor he would expect from a woman with far less strength and wit than he suspected Jane had. And if that were the case, why did she always pretend to be uninteresting and superficial?

One of the downsides to living in the middle of a barely-inhabited desert was that a drive to the nearest big town was quite long, which Jane would understand, but would also leave them in each other's company for a significant amount of time. He wondered if Jane would keep up the act or drop her guard. His instincts told him to be prepared for anything.

After a few minutes of silence, Jane suddenly became fidgety, making a show of tapping her fingers and looking for things in her purse.

"Do you like to listen to music?" she asked. Cundo almost laughed.

"Yeah, what do you want to listen to?"

Jane flipped through the screen on his console, scanning the selection of music provided by the bluetooth connection to his phone. He waited to hear her verdict impatiently, knowing that someone like her probably judged a person's music choices harshly.

"Wow, there's quite a...variety in here."

"Yeah, I guess I don't know what I like."

"I know what you like," she replied cryptically, and stopped on a song. He kept his eyes on the road, but his peripheral vision caught something that made his hair stand on end.

And then she started the music.

The instrumentals started up and a feminine doo-wop began in the background. A chill ran down his spine and he forced himself to remain focused on the road before his vehicle, squinting against the low sun. The music paused for just a moment before Paul Anka's voice swept in with a full, reverberating romance.

"Put your head on my...sho-oulde-er..."

Jane began to hum alone.

"Hold me in your arms..."

She watched him, humming.

"Ba-aby..."

Cundo's hands tightened on his steering wheel. He wasn't sure if she was trying to make him uneasy or if it was his natural reaction to hearing the song his mother had sung in his youth. Memories tugged at his senses and threatened to take over, but he kept a tight grip on reality by focusing on the soft, full sound of Jane's voice. She sang smilingly, obviously aware of the effect the song had on him, but seemingly unaware of the effect her voice had. It was nothing like his mother's wind-chime voice, the voice that had graced church choirs and Christmas caroling groups in town squares. Jane's was more like the voice you heard echoing in a steamy shower, wondering where the mystical sound originated from.

Now he was thinking about Jane in the shower.

They finally, after what seemed like a painful, five-hour drive, arrived at the small town theatre. He rushed around to her side to help her out, but had to pause at the sight of one, smooth leg outstretched, prepared to use the step down...ending in a shiny pink heel covered in spikes. Her calves flexed, her foot arching into the heel that he hadn't noticed before, steel spikes looking both terrifying and inviting at the same time.

He fought the urge to cup her calves and run his hands down to grasp her ankles. Instead, he reached for her hand and took her down in a polite grip. She gave him a smile meant to disarm and he absorbed it like a punch, leaning on his military stoicism to avoid showing any reaction. She obviously intended to ruffle his feathers and she sorely needed to be taught who Cundo truly was. He was not a bird, and before her arrival, he could not be ruffled.

The movie theatre was a hub of activity for the younger community. The small building with its worn arcade games and threadbare theatre upholstery did not inspire thoughts of decadence and virility, but the young people of the town gathered there to socialize and wear their trendiest outfits. The theatre and the nearby drive-in restaurant were where the sparse community of teens appeared. One of the appeals that West Texas held for Cundo was the lack of nightlife and the older, retiring community that did not exhaust him with constant, irrational activity.

"You bitch!" a laughing voice squealed, drawing their attention to an air hockey table in the arcade center where two girls in bleached, denim shorts abused the puck with their meager skills of coordination. Cundo fought tension in his jaw and pushed Jane along to the concession and ticket counter, ignoring the way she stiffened at the feel of his hand on her back.

"Two for the seven pm of Bloody Summer Nights, please," he muttered at the freckled teen wearing the striped theatre uniform. The teen scrambled to catch the cash Cundo tossed at him and punched away at his computer wordlessly. Jane watched Cundo like he was the most fascinating specimen. He hated it. He wanted to stare at her and see if she liked it. He doubted she would.

"Interesting choice," she commented as they walked away. In retaliation, Cundo returned his hand to the small of her back, watching her face firm up with grim satisfaction.

"It was the only thing out that wasn't a sequel."

The theatre was already pitch black when they walked in, and Cundo turned his good eye to the little numbers on the rows. He paused to look closer, but Jane tugged him along to their seats without stopping. She plopped herself down in her seat confidently, the little flair of her dress riding up, revealing flawless thighs. Cundo was suddenly aware of the intimacy of a dark theatre and close seats. His clothes felt too tight.

As the curtains widened to accommodate the projection on the screen, Cundo felt the pricking of awareness on the back of his neck. The screen lit up with the parental warning, and Cundo questioned for the first time if this was a wise choice for a movie. The trailer had seemed fairly gruesome, and he may very well have the wrong idea about Jane. Perhaps there wasn't a hardened shell of malicious intent under her filmy little dress, and he'd been imagining threats that weren't there...he did that for months after retiring from service. He was used to calming his paranoia and developing apathy, but he simply couldn't when it came to Jane. If she hated the movie or screamed in terror, he would whisk her away.

Around ten minutes into the movie, Jane surprised him. He should have expected it, but he didn't. Instead of being disturbed by the gore in the film as she stated she would be, she giggled at the exaggerated, B-movie effects, remaining stock still when a jump-scare occurred except to emit a derisive snort. Cundo found himself watching her instead of the screen, fascinated by the unnatural expressions she made. When she thought he wasn't looking, she let her shields drop, and her reactions to everything around her conflicted with that of the rest of the audience. At one point, a child opened the emergency exit instead of leaving out of the theatre door, and the sharp, unexpected light of the sunset caused half of the audience to scream. Jane, on the other hand, leaned forward with an almost gleeful look on her face, and fell back with mild disappointment when it seemed no dangerous intrusion was afoot.

As the movie came to a close, the male and female lead showed a predictable yet un-foreshadowed romantic interest in one another. The man leaned in to gently press his hand to a wound in the woman's shoulder, and suddenly they were passionately embracing one another. Cundo awkwardly flickered his gaze to Jane, and found her staring at him. She looked conflicted, her head tilted slightly, big, pretty eyes narrowed with a seriousness that opposed the whimsy of her appearance. Cundo felt observed again, and a sudden desire to agitate her arose.

"Are you wondering what it would feel like to kiss me?" he whispered gruffly.

Jane seemed to be startled out of her reverie, realizing how close their faces were, and looked at him with a cocked brow before responding.

"You'd be pleased to hear that, wouldn't you?"

"No," he returned carefully, keeping his voice low even though the lights were brightening and the credits were rolling. "I just assume that you're concerned how the scars would feel against your face." She didn't flinch.

"Well, how do they feel on your own?"

It shouldn't have felt like an insult, but it did.

Cundo pulled Jane out of her seat by her arm, gentling his touch by folding her palm over the crook of his elbow, like they were entering a ballroom instead of leaving a musty old theatre.

They didn't speak when they got in the car, and they didn't speak during the drive back. Jane found another song that made his skin crawl and sang it as he navigated gravel roads in the twilight. He didn't ask about kissing her again.

Cundo walked Jane to her door but kept a respectable distance, aware of how proximity could make a woman feel. Jane twirled around in her dangerous heels and gave him an even more dangerous smile.

"I had so much fun tonight, thank you for taking me out."

"Are you sure?"

She looked at him queerly.

"Of course I am, silly," she seemed exasperated with him, and he wondered if she simply wanted to go inside and was waiting for him to leave. He couldn't leave without irritating her one more time.

Slowly taking her hand, he picked it up and pressed it against his chest. She didn't want to be touched- he understood that. But some new part of him wanted to feel her hands on him, right over where his heart beat- loud and demanding.

She stood stock still, her mouth parted and her hand frozen in his. He watched her.

"I-"

"Listen," she interrupted him, pulling her hand from his swiftly. He felt the absence of her warmth immediately. "I don't think I can do this again. I'm sorry, I've just never dated someone with…"

She paused to feign embarrassment, but her eyes didn't change.

"With a face like yours."

He reared back, feeling as though he'd been slapped. If it hadn't been for the following look of satisfaction on her face, he would have believed her.

"Oh yeah?"

"Yes," she said with false pity on her tongue. "It's hard to look at you. It's…it's frightening, really. I'm sorry."

Cundo felt nothing but a low boiling of fury rising in his stomach. Had anyone else uttered those words, it would have simply confirmed for him what he felt about himself. It would have been crushing, but understandable. But something about the way Jane said it- something about the way her eyes remained on him, steady and unflinching, not even bothering to look at his scars as she talked about them…nothing made Cundo angrier than dishonesty.

"You don't owe me an explanation," he finally said, watching her try to cover up her surprise. "But for the record, I would appreciate the truth more than a lie."

She opened her mouth to respond, but he put up his hand, the same one that could still feel hers in it.

"Don't worry. I get it. I'll leave you alone."

Cundo turned before she could make something else up and disappeared into the darkness behind his headlights.

Jane waited until she couldn't see his truck anymore before flinging open her door and storming angrily inside.

"I would appreciate the truth…"

The truth. Jane hadn't told the truth in years. The truth was something her father had valued, but it had become something she could not afford.

She looked down at the hand she was grasping. The hand that had been pressed against Cundo's massive, stone-hard chest.

She could still feel his heart beating hard and fast against her palm. The disturbing comparison between his heartbeat and that of her victims felt heavy in her mind. She couldn't help but visualize her first prey, a college-aged boy with sweaty, meaty hands and dirty fingernails. She tried to calm herself by remembering the steps she'd taken, calm and cool despite her lack of experience. It always brought her peace to remember those moments.

The adrenaline of her first kill wasn't enough to shut off her fear of being discovered. She'd planned for some time, but many things went wrong. There were too many nights after that she'd feared she'd wake up to the authorities at her door, but the case was closed. Like most of her prey, she'd set him up to be "killed in an unfortunate accident." She'd let the budding sexual predator who had accosted her on campus after dark "fall" down a very steep set of concrete stairs. She'd been out for blood, desperately wanting to stop him before he inevitably turned into the type of monster that abused her in the foster system. After a semester of learning a great deal about sexual abuse and assault and the mindset of predators in her psychology classes, she felt that this was more about research, more for academic purposes, than about violence. But something else in her knew that it was also for justice- she knew that no one would stop him if she did not.

So she'd lured him out to the stairwell in the blindspot of campus security cameras, and she took him by surprise. She fully expected to have to hit him with the metal pipe she'd brought that she'd ensured was the same size as the railing, but he broke his neck at the bottom of the staircase. His eyes had been wide open, and she'd pressed her fingers to his corroded artery to await the stillness that would signify his death, but she found herself pressing her hand to his chest, some primal part of her needing to feel his heart stop. Those final moments were inspiring, arousing, life-changing, and she felt his heart thud to a halting end like a tragic, caged animal. She'd tipped her head back in ecstasy when she realized that she'd succeeded.

But tonight, Cundo had taken her hand and forced her to realize that he was alive, and worse, forced her to realize that he was someone she could never kill.

Her hand vibrated with the memory of his heartbeat, and she desperately tore into the kitchen in search of something to stop her from feeling it. She ripped a santoku knife from the block of knives on the counter, fishing for a lighter.

He couldn't distract her, he couldn't derail her carefully laid plans. Jane simply couldn't let this man be different from anyone else- anyone is potential prey, she thought hysterically, her hands shaking as she stroked the flame of the lighter up and down the blade.

Anyone is fair game. He's not different. Anyone can be a monster. Even he can be a monster. She may very well have to kill him one day.

When the knife was glowing and she smelt residue burning and smoking off of the knife, she dropped the lighter and pressed the hot blade against her palm, the very palm that could not shake the sensation of Cundo's beating heart.

She roared in frustration until her throat burned as much as her hand, and didn't let go of the blade until hot tears rolled down her face, until she miserably realized that the imprint of Cundo's touch was permanently tattooed into her palm.

CHAPTER 7

Tasmanian Devil, Sarcophilus harrisil

Neon lights reflected in the oily puddles of rainwater between buildings. Jane let her heavy boots sink into the potholes, kicking up diamonds of water into the air. She was feeling dangerous this evening, having spent the past couple of days putting her investigation on hold. The resources Lasica had given her had fallen flat, giving her no further leads that she had not already discovered for herself. Tonight, she had taken matters into her own hands, shoving her hair up into a cap and inquiring around the three cop bars scattered across the bordering towns around Zemsta. It had taken her hours, but the small notebook in the pocket of her denim jacket was filled to the brim with words that drunk, retired men wouldn't remember saying the next morning. Rumors about her father and a leak on the force, names and dates and exaggerated facts.

The alleyways she strutted down were the kinds of places young women were told not to be found in, but Jane was not a young woman, she was a predator. An apex predator, the kind that other predators should fear.

That was the thought that was on her mind when she saw the shadow stretch out before her, parallel to her own. The fall of the person's feet were heavy and even, men's feet, deliberately on pace with her own. She caught the reflection of him behind her in a restaurant window to her left, and despite the fact that his hands were in his pockets and his head was down, she knew that his eyeline could easily raise to take in her entire figure.

He was too close.

Instead of feeling titillated at the prospect of a kill in the midst of her dry spell, she felt tired. She didn't have any leftover energy to stage this man's fatal accident, to learn about his life from his wallet, to create a suicide or a mugging. She simply didn't have it this evening.

But he wasn't letting up. She deliberately led him deeper and deeper down paths of chain link fences and discarded furniture behind abandoned strip malls, deeper into areas that would not be populated or under the eye of a security camera...places that he would feel safe in. She should leave, follow the streetlamps, walk into a populated establishment, scream, or outrun him with her carefully-developed muscles...

But she didn't.

Jane walked with light, unconcerned steps, and the anonymous man behind her followed. He must be stupid, she thought. But that was okay. Stupid people could be monsters, too.

He grew close enough that she could feel the air he moved, and just as she heard the rustle of his coat as he reached for her, she dipped out of the way, turning, feet spread apart, boots firmly planted in preparation for a fight. She was tired, but her frustration was amping up her thirst. Perhaps one anonymous kill would help tonight.

He moved quicker than she expected, and pulled a switchblade from his back pocket. Nice, dull, non-criminals don't often carry switchblades. Her lips twitched, but she didn't want to reveal anything on her face. She wanted him to be surprised.

And surprised he was.

Her body moved with the fluidity of someone that had practiced the disarming techniques of Aikido many times. Her father had taught her how to disarm someone and relieve them of any weapon, but she had furthered her education herself, learning how to become her own weapon, and make one out of anything.

Sexual predators were not prepared for prey that fought- they were sharks, they wanted a bite without a fight. One punch to the gills usually sent them swimming away. But sometimes, they got angry.

Anonymous was getting angry tonight. It looked like he was willing to settle for difficult prey.

I am not prey.

Within a few short seconds, Jane was in possession of the man's knife, and she wasn't ignorant of what to do with it. Anonymous was worked up enough to continue advancing, swinging for her head in the hopes that his fist could reach her before his knife could reach his gut.

He had miscalculated.

Jane snorted in derision at the astonishment on the man's scruffy face. Though she would typically aim for a faster, more efficiently fatal part of the anatomy, the abdominal area was common amongst thieves and muggers in back alleys. She made sure to cock her wrist at an angle that didn't reveal her height as the attacker, twisting and pulling it out with a practiced hand as he drifted to the ground. She watched his face, excited despite her exhaustion to see how his mask of death would manifest.

His blood flowed freely between her fingers, and she kept her body angled away to avoid blood splatter on her clothes. Her mouth was uncontrollable this time, and she smiled as the warmth cascaded over her wrist. The dim light in his eyes dimmed further and went out completely, leaving Jane in the darkness behind a dumpster and an abandoned, molding couch. A sense of peace settled over her as her body accepted that she was finally alone, and that the threat had been neutralized.

Using her unbloodied hand to pull on cotton medical gloves, she reveled in the instant quietness of her mind. Why had she gone so long without killing? Every part of her had clearly desperately needed it.

Jane removed the contents of the man's jeans pockets, and pulled off both boots. She turned them over, confirming their emptiness, and divested his wallet of all cash and cards. When she pulled the last of the cash out, something lighter than money fluttered to the ground.

The picture landed face up, and Jane didn't bother crouching to retrieve it. The face of a young girl stared up at her, and although she would like to believe that it was a souvenir from a victim, the likeness between her newest prey and the stranger in the picture was unignorable. Whether this was an old picture of a sister, or perhaps a niece...God forbid, a daughter...Jane couldn't stop to think about it. Efficiency was key.

She scanned the scene for any trace of herself. Efficiency is key...don't think about the girl. The cash, cards, knife, and gloves went into a bag in her jacket pocket...efficiency...she couldn't stop thinking. She pulled the man's pockets inside out and scattered his wallet and belongings about.

Her hands grew hot and she avoided looking at the fresh corpse on the ground. What would they tell his family? What would the little girl do? Would she go into foster care?

Efficiency is key…

The crackle of the fire amidst the ring of stones in Jane's backyard helped settle her nerves. She'd hoped that they'd stay settled after taking a fresh life, perhaps even feel a bit invigorated. Instead, all she could feel was Cundo's heartbeat under her fingers, and see the face of the young girl from the picture flashing before her eyes.

Jane stoked the fire in front of her and threw her cotton medical gloves on the fire that had just melted and burned the anonymous man's amenities. She didn't look at the name on the card. It was best if she didn't know his name, especially in the unusual state she was in now. She went back to unscrewing the pieces of his switchblade and pulling it apart. She would melt the plastic part of the handle into some cold water and then flake it apart. The metal she would bleach, scorch, and hammer until it didn't resemble anything and throw it on a pile of scrap metal. She was nothing if not detail-oriented.

Looking up at the cloud-veiled stars, Jane pulled a deep breath in through the scarf wrapped around her face, keeping out the toxic fumes from the cards.

To distract her cluttered mind from the thoughts she couldn't quite process, she retrieved her laptop from her father's old desk that she'd placed back in it's corner of the living room. She was typically careful with her research, but given the innocent interest she'd already shown, she figured that using her own computer and a public search engine wouldn't be as dangerous. If anything, it would establish a digital trail that she was cyber-stalking a flame during the general TOD of the anonymous man behind the strip mall.

That's what she told herself as she pulled up the veteran's database.

Facundo Del Sur, she typed into the search bar for the service records.

CHAPTER 8

West African Lungfish, Protopterus annectens

Facundo pulled his monstrous Ford into the parking lot in front of the bank. The town square was the kind of place that showed up inexplicably in Hallmark movies, the place where unfortunate tourists gathered to get the "small town" effect without having to actually encroach on the wilderness. For Cundo, it was a location where outsiders could potentially gawk at his scars.

But today was not the day to think about Jane's cruel words, or to determine whether or not she meant them. Today was a Wednesday, and that meant one very specific thing.

The great thing about Wednesdays was that he could put his military training to use and plan strategically. Most importantly- he could think about absolutely nothing else. Single mindedness was not Cundo's strong suit. Not until his mother's death.

His target emerged from a clean, white SUV, and skipped into the bank. Cundo remained behind the tinted windows of his vehicle.

13:00.

He emerged. Cundo twisted on his cowboy hat and followed him discreetly.

13:10.

The man arrived at the shop several doors down that sold goat cheese and locally sourced soaps. Cundo ducked into the shop just past it to avoid suspicion. He examined things in the window to watch out for the man, and when he emerged with a paper bag, Cundo made some notes on a small flip book before thrusting it back in his pocket and tipping his hat at the clerk and exiting.

13:35.

There was a post office around the block. The man chose to stroll there, it was a nice day for Zemsta. Only 85 degrees.

Cundo followed.

The back of the man's head was familiarly shaped, light, thinning hair shaved close to the head. Block-shaped, short neck, narrow shoulders. Easier to look at than his face. Cundo knew it well. He'd watched it every other Wednesday, he'd followed him from a distance and watched as he went about his day. Cundo knew the back of this man's head better than he knew his own face. His silhouette haunted his dreams, his left shoulder starred in his nightmares. Every move this man made was a reminder to Cundo that he was capable of killing.

The short, thinning hair on the man's head glistened with sweat. The back of his neck was tomato-red, and Cundo searched for a sign that he was struggling, straining in some way that did not make him the antagonist of the story unfolding before him.

But the thick, meaty hands that wrapped around his mother's throat held no sign of hesitation. His mother was clearly already dead, her eyes having bulged, the capillaries bursting and spreading red in her bright, beautiful eyes. Her mouth open, tongue breaching her lips in a grotesque parody of childlike mocking. Cundo could not move. The beast with his hands around his mother's neck let her go, her body crumpling to the floor like a ragdoll. Unceremonious, an irreverent end to her tragically short life.

When the beast turned, he was not the huffing, repulsive monster of Cundo's nightmares to come. He was a sweat-slicked man with a round face and too-red lips that gasped with the exertion of strangling a woman. He looked surprised, like he hadn't planned on killing her. His close-set eyes widened at the image of Cundo, scrawny and seventeen, standing in his way. He simply looked at the boy and turned, throwing open the window behind him and punching through the screen to escape.

It all ended very quickly. Cundo didn't chase him; he wouldn't even know what to do if he caught him. He simply sat on the ground beside his mother's slight, lifeless body. The beast never returned to the house. Not to gather his things or retrieve any money. Not to remove any evidence of the sin he committed against his short-term engagement to the beautiful Tiguan woman he'd met in California. He didn't return to defend his reputation when the local news spread his picture far and wide, or when his ex-soon-to-be stepson was delivered to his ex-soon-to-be in-laws...an orphan.

The beast simply didn't return. And Cundo returned every night to that little room in the beast's home where his mother lay, newly dead, and thought and thought and thought. When he awoke from his nightmares, he kept thinking. When he joined the military so that he would no longer have to be an independent thinker who was plagued with the burden of his mother's unavenged murder, he still thought.

The beast didn't show up when Cundo retired and made friends with local law-enforcement. He didn't show up until Cundo had dug up the conspiracies about his mother's murder and developed theories and become freshly furious and thought and thought and thought and thought.

The beast didn't return until Cundo was ready.

As if the very devil was satisfied that he was prepared to take his mother's life back through the throat of the beast that killed her.

Cundo held back in the line at the post office, prepared to grumble in an even lower voice to the postmaster, asking for some stamps. The line ahead of him was a continuous replica of him; men in cowboy hats and dusty boots. The hatless head of the man at the front of the line held Cundo's entire attention. So much so, that he did not notice when a separate head entered the small post office vestibule.

Golden curls awry, orchid-skinned face aflame, surprise colored her face at seeing him, but it was replaced with frustration so quickly, that it looked like Jane had arrived at the post office solely to give him a dressing-down.

Shit.

He turned, blocking her body from the line of people and hustled her out of the door before she could utter a word. He didn't stop pushing her, to her frazzled astonishment, until they'd exited the building completely.

Around the corner of the building, Cundo held Jane by the shoulder with one hand, and whipped his hat off with the other. Once again, the sight of his scars caused no physical reaction in her. Suddenly, she pulled in a breath and leaned forward, as if to shout.

"FACUNDO LOCK-"

He slapped a hand over her mouth, burying his guilt at the sound it made.

"Hush," he whispered harshly, removing his hand slowly.

"Why exactly do you have a different last name now? What are you hiding?"

Cundo watched her carefully, looking at her uncharacteristically disheveled appearance. She wore none of the delicate, fragile sundresses and little shoes that made him suspicious of her. Her sensible boots and denim jacket seemed like a secret that she was revealing to him, and it almost made him smile.

She'd been researching him.

His smile dropped.

"How do you know my real last name?"

"I looked you up," she bit out. "You're a liar, Mr. Locklear. Who are you exactly?"

"I'm not Locklear anymore," he replied, even and honest. "My name was changed legally."

"After your services? What is the purpose of that?"

They stared at each other.

"It was easier."

"What was easier?"

"You couldn't understand."

She'd already ruined his observations for the day, so Cundo jammed his hat back on his rumpled hair, and simply said "And quite frankly, it's none of your business." before turning to get back in his truck.

"Oh, I don't think so," she hissed, following him. He ignored her, but she climbed into the passenger seat of his car before he could lock the doors.

"You don't get to tell me I won't understand something and then storm off."

"Why, because that's your thing?"

Jane threw up her hands, and Cundo strongly considered reaching past her to open the door and shove her out.

"No, because I'm not the sort of person that you can deceive and not experience consequences," she responded rather quietly. He hadn't expected that reply.

"Well, I guess you'll have to get used to it."

"Are you here for me." It wasn't really a question. She was watching him evenly, and he noticed for the first time that her familiar leather bag was slung over her shoulder. Despite the oddity of her question, his mind was turning down an unwanted lane, led by the mane of golden curls tumbling around her shoulders and down. He followed their wild trail, and almost got lost until Jane leaned forward, drawing his eyes up to hers.

"Are you?"

Cundo didn't know how to respond to that.

"What the hell are you talking about?"

"What do you know about me?" She answered quickly.

"Nothing!" he replied honestly, fed up with her interrogation. She couldn't possibly believe that she had the right to be suspicious of him after her insult to him, and the sudden interruption of what she had to have thought was his daily errands. "All I know is that you're an annoying brat who either follows me around town into my place of work or my car, only to be a bitch once you have my attention."

She jerked back, and he felt a bit smug that he'd finally thrown her off balance. He wasn't sure why, but he wanted to blurt out the truth.

"I changed my name because it was plastered all over the news, not once, but twice, and I'm done being someone else's entertainment. Even yours, Miss Fairweather. So if you don't mind-" before he could shove her out of the car, she interrupted.

"Because of your mom?" Of course she knew. If she'd looked for his name, she'd found the articles.

"And because of the accident?"

He didn't want her to know any of this.

He didn't want her in his car.

"Get out."

He thought she'd put up more of a fight, but she simply climbed out of the vehicle and stood off to the side as he peeled out of the parking lot and disappeared before he could attract the attention of his target.

It wasn't until he got home that he realized where he'd seen a purse like hers before. It was a concealed-carry purse.

CHAPTER 9

Wildcat, Felis silvestris

"There are just some things...I've tried to pretend...I just can't ignore them anymore-"

"You're worried for nothing, Maria, what are they saying? You know I'd never hurt you."

"It's not me that I'm worried about, Phil..."

"It's because you're a damn gossip, you and those women at church!"

"I just want to know where the rumors came from, just tell me-"

Cundo strained to hear the conversation through the thin walls of the California condo, but the following sentences didn't make sense to him. His mom was getting angry, calling Phil names that he'd only ever heard whispered between other boys at school. The kinds of things that parents try not to talk to their kids about, try not to scare them with.

The shouting came to a climax and suddenly it was only Phil shouting. He'd never seen him get angry before, but Cundo was protective over his mother, and suspicious of the men who molested her with their eyes in public. Just because Maria Locklear had decided to give Phil a chance didn't mean that he was allowed to be cruel to her. Cundo made the decision to intervene, but by the time he opened the door to their bedroom, his mother wasn't there. Just a body.

Facundo lifted his glass until the amber liquid disappeared into a burning path down his throat. The anniversary of his mother's death was always a struggle to deal with, but in previous years, he'd had people to answer to, enemy fire to avoid, and injuries to recover from. Last year, he escaped by building up his business. This year, he was still. There was nothing to distract him from the memories that swarmed in like wasps, stinging away at his peace and silence.

He had hoped to feel a sense of purpose following Phil yesterday. It always helped keep the demons at bay, like he was feeding them just a little bit. He never talked to him, he always kept his distance. He'd done everything right, keeping his presence a secret. A couple of times in the past year, Phil had wandered into The Red Light, and Cundo simply made himself busy with something in his office and tried not to think about the man's hands all over his bar. He promised himself that he'd do something one of these days, that he'd had a purpose other than owning a bar when he came to this town.

He told himself he'd put his mother's soul to rest.

Cundo brought the box from his dresser to his reading chair, and opened it with his non-whiskey-grasping hand. The box squeaked open and revealed the pictures of him and his mother, weighed down by the heavy, beaded bracelet. He picked it up and rubbed his finger along one of the beads, the stone rough where he'd worn the glaze down. He set the bracelet aside and pulled out the photos, which were yellowing, the film peeling off of the surface. He stroked a finger over his mother's fine-boned face, smiling at whoever was taking the picture. She was wearing oversized jeans and white sneakers, her straight hair pulled back into her signature braid. In her thin arms was a little boy, chubby cheeks and night-black eyes. The baby looked like he was on the verge of a smile, mouth open, tiny hand raised in the air. Soft, flawless skin...waiting to be marred years later.

This was how Cundo prefered to remember his mother- youthful, blissfully happy, and completely in control of her life. Although she'd had Cundo rather young, and didn't have enough of a relationship with his father to rely on him, Maria Locklear had been intent upon building a life for herself and her son without help. Everything would have been fine if it hadn't been for Phil.

Philip Caruthers.

The name stood out on the stark white of the paper he held. Buried under the photos, he'd kept his secret intel; pictures and papers of evidence that pieced together the life of the man that had disappeared one fateful night in Sacramento, California, and turned into someone else completely. It was easy to disappear when everything you had to your name was already someone else's. Mr. Caruthers had been brought in on identity theft and insurance fraud more than once. He'd made a comfortable bed of embezzled money from somewhere on the east coast right before he met Maria Locklear and her young son. They were easy targets.

They were going to secure his facade, make it easier to blend in, but Maria wasn't stupid. She'd discovered some of Phil's secrets...the worst ones.

Cundo had yet to find out what those secrets were, but he planned to use them as soon as the man was within his grasp. As soon as he had more evidence that Phil and the man he was stalking were the same person, and that his crimes had not stopped the night his mother's pulse did, Cundo would destroy him.

That's what his plan had been before.

Things were getting difficult. He felt an itch from the inside out, a sickening urge to leave his house and run as fast as he could, run Phil down like a cheetah, run until he could pounce and catch Phil in his claws and swing him to the ground. Then he'd crush the man's throat between his powerful jaws, and the last thing his prey would see would be the mottled scars running the length of Cundo's face.

He couldn't stop thinking about it.

The conflict between himself and Jane had been a welcome distraction, but it only made him wilder, took him further from the rest he'd earned after his service. There were days when he wondered if he even deserved a rest.

Among the papers that had to do with Phil, there was an address. It hadn't been difficult to find, he'd simply listened in on his conversations with the postmaster. Criminals should really be more careful, but a small town like this offered a layer of protection. It was a combination of hiding in plain sight as well as being surrounded by unsuspecting people. He'd also discreetly recorded a conversation Phil had had with a clerk at the bank, relaying his previous addresses...one of which was the home he'd briefly moved into with his mother. Happy memories, falsified, like Phil's records.

That recording alone was proof enough to re-open the case of his mother's death.

And yet here he sat.

He'd been stalking Phil for weeks, stoking his anger until he started thinking irrational things.

He couldn't commit a crime. He'd done too much in the service; he'd hurt and been hurt, and there were many times when he wasn't sure if he'd ever come back home. His mother was dead, and he'd survived war. She would hate it if he wasted what was left of his life for her, especially with her already in the ground. But how could he let this go…how could he let this man exist?

He should call the police.

He should kill him.

No, he should deliver this information to the authorities.

He is the authorities.

Damn.

Cundo held onto his mother's bracelet.

Jane deftly flipped through the cheap, narrow canvases propped up in the thrifted firewood rack. She stared down at her early abstract pieces and wondered at their chaos. She'd forgotten what she'd been looking for, swept away on a wave of memories.

The first time she'd used art as an outlet was when one of her foster mothers, a children's counselor, had taken her to a class that used painting to explore bottled-up emotions. She'd been offended by the suggestion, knowing that "troubled kids" were the ones that attended these things, but when she arrived, and her foster mother had put the brush in her hand, she instantly knew that she'd found something to love. Painting was safe, and safety was hard to come by as a foster kid.

Although she couldn't take that particular foster mom with her, she took her love of art. Her paintings had gone from being emotional, abstract pieces from the heart of a lonely teen, to the calculating oils done in college, transforming dramatically after her first kill. That first time had been clumsy but glorious, and the painting she'd made, a carefully-hidden piece that showed the urban landscape that was her scene of the crime, was equally so. These days her pieces were experimental, confusing even to her. She tinkered with chemicals to see what made texture and color. No matter what, she could not seem to recreate the authenticity of her first pieces. Perhaps she had simply expended that ability, and she was now empty.

Empty.

That's how her pieces looked. They were void of warmth, void of life. A mockery of the woman that created them. She grew angry as she looked at the pieces, organized by time frame, and felt her eyes burn with frustration at the evidence of her emptiness. She wanted to be a grand painter, to somehow have the emotional ability to create art without the complications such abilities caused outside her art studio. She wanted to be empty everywhere but here.

Not for the first time, Jane wondered what her father might think of her. Would he be proud of his daughter for being an unstoppable vigilante, using everything he taught her and more to be the best? Or would he think her a monster, no better than her prey?

Jane dropped the canvases back into order with a thud and buried her thoughts. She already knew the answer. She was a predator in the night, a repugnant creature that found satisfaction in bloodshed. She was an expendable life that made nothing better other than reducing statistics by an infinitesimal amount.

Grabbing a jar of paintbrushes and some industrial-sized bottles of paint, she wandered back to the large canvas she'd set up in the dusty, backyard plot. Her mother had once made an oasis of this space, but Jane had not the time nor the patience to recreate it. Instead, she decided, she would paint what her mother had once coaxed out of lifeless earth.

Greens, blues, reds, browns, yellows, white, titanium white, cotton white, some more green, spring this time, add more dandelion to the evergreen, and throw a heather-grey in it to dull it down. Layer in bits of verdant green, some reptile green, some chemical green, tamper it back down with creams and eggshells and peaches and strawberries. A conch color, a coral color, the color of grapefruit and hibiscus and prickly pears. All bursting out of a ground made of coffee beans and sienna, dust and earth. Rich browns made of chocolate and raw ones made of tanned hide. Manipulating and moving and smoothing with palette knives. The canvas croaked in protest if the paint became too thin, the knife scraping across, and Jane would mix and splatter and pour and layer until the knife glided across smoothly, like a hand over the surface of a still pond.

Jane became so entranced by her painting that for a moment, she almost didn't feel her hunger. Her physical hunger, oh that was gone. Her eyes, gone raw with staying open late into the evening, straining against lamplight, felt no fatigue. But her mind still held onto a corner of the hunger she felt for prey.

Even now, elbow-deep in acrylic, she couldn't keep the thoughts at bay. They were the only thing that caught her attention when she was entrenched in her paintings. Her last prey had not been enough, and she had had to snip off the satisfaction of the scene in order to get rid of the infected thoughts-the guilt that came in the form of a little photograph of a girl smiling. She needed a clean scene, one with no strings and no casualties.

She would need to kill soon.

CHAPTER 10

Emerald Tree Boa, Corallus caninus

It had been very sudden, her finding her next prey. She'd been laying low in the investigation of her father's killer when she'd decided to attend some local events.

T-ball.

She wouldn't have thought to go herself, having no interests in sports or untalented children that she had no connection to, but she'd overheard word of it at the post office, and decided to attend. Women didn't stand out when attending events for kids alone, though a man would. She could mingle with the proud mothers and unlock town secrets with compliments on their children's amatuer baseball skills. There was also the added bonus of being able to spot a sexual predator amongst the attendees. She was confident that she could do so without much trouble, and satiate her unstoppable hunger while searching for information on her own case.

"Good afternoon, ma'am," chirped the pleasantly rotund woman at the makeshift gate in front of the stands. The baseball diamond for the little ones was made up of cones and set within a soccer field. The parents gathered on the bottom rows of the stadium, prepared to cheer on tiny people wielding tiny bats.

"Good afternoon," Jane returned in an equally chipper tone. Handing her a dollar- a voluntary donation to the team in exchange for a ticket- she entered the sacred space that smelt of gatorade, peanuts, and innocence. Predators were not allowed within these confines, but the same dangerous hunger in Jane that made her want to kill men made her feel welcome in a place meant only for those who could be victims. She felt like an invisible, avenging angel guarding the entrance to a dormitory filled with innocents. She was one of them once, but now she couldn't be victimized even with both hands tied behind her back. She'd done too much to retain the title of "prey".

Among the hot, aluminum seats, parents- wearing home-made t-shirts celebrating their child's imaginary allegiance to a team- held smaller children and kept the heat at bay with personal fans and insulated cups. She suspected that some of these parents were smart enough to keep something stronger than sweet tea in their cups.

A whistle blew and an announcer came over the intercom, which turned out to be someone with a karaoke machine speaking into the microphone at the top of the stands.

He announced the switching of the teams, and Jane lost track of her perusal of the crowd to examine the ritual happening on the field. She'd been to sports events for foster brothers and sisters before, and there were plenty of track meets attended by her father in her youth, but she hadn't been around children very much since she was one. These tiny creatures were much smaller than her memory of elementary school served. Some of them only came up to the coaches' knees. She watched with uncomfortable concern as one of the team members stamped the ground and pulled off his helmet when he missed the ball sitting atop the t-ball stand. The "umpire" crouching behind him offered him a hug, which seemed to dissipate some of the tears, but he was still upset and refused to swing again. From the sidelines, a coach wearing a blue t-shirt and white shorts urged the boy to return to the stand. The parents in the stands cheered as the boy took an uncoordinated swing at the ball at the encouragement of the coach. He hit the ball and it tumbled surprisingly far from him. The coach leaned down and whispered something in the boy's ear. The boy stood still and simply walked back to his bench when he was done, not bothering to celebrate his success. Jane wondered.

She wasn't sure how long baseball games usually lasted, but she figured it was best to begin as soon as possible. She approached the family that had been cheering the loudest and gave her best impression of a bashful baseball fan.

"Hi! Is that your little boy?" Jane asked the mom, pointing out at the field but pulling her hand back to give a quick wave to the baby in her arms. The baby watched her with wide eyes.

"Yes! That's our little one, Morgan," the mother said proudly, exchanging a contented smile with the man next to her. "This is my husband, Morgan Senior."

Her husband nodded at Jane, and she reached over to give him a gentle handshake, keeping her eyes on the little bundle in the mother's arms.

"He's got quite an arm on him!" Jane quipped, looking back at the field. The boy had taken the helmet off his curly head once more and was sitting on the edge of his bench, away from his peers. His mother beamed.

"Here, have a seat," the mother said. Jane was almost hesitant. These people were far too trusting. The woman scooched down the bench and moved the diaper bag from beside her. "My name is Lindsey."

"Thanks! My name's Jane. I was wondering how the team was doing, my niece was supposed to be playing for the other team today, but they already headed out." Jane tilted her head and gave a sympathetic shrug. "The allergies always get her this time of year."

"Aw, poor baby," Lindsey said, and offered Jane some of her kettle corn.

Jane struck up a conversation with the trusting Lindsey and Morgan Senior, and quickly learned just about every detail of their lives. Morgan Junior was adopted as an infant, and Jane felt a twinge of empathy towards the boy, wondering what his life was like before his adoption. Clearly his new family was loving, but the journey on his way to them couldn't have been easy. She understood.

Their new baby, Patty, reached out and grasped her fingers together in midair, her chubby hands reaching for Jane as her mother described Morgan's foster care prior to the adoption process.

"I was a foster kid," Jane said distantly, distracted by the baby's pudgy fist, which had clasped around one of the locks of curls coming loose from her braid. She wasn't sure why she said it, but she felt safe around this woman. She hadn't often hoped to be adopted when she was in the system, but if she'd been adopted by a family like this, perhaps her life would've been different.

"Oh, wow! Then you understand our boy," Lindsey said with another winning smile. She adjusted Patty's baby hat so that it further shielded her eyes from the sun. "He had a hard time with his health for the first few months, his mom couldn't stop using during her pregnancy. But you know, kids are resilient."

Jane bristled at that.

"Although they shouldn't have to be."

Then she softened.

She'd heard that phrase too many times before, her social worker reassuring foster families that she wasn't broken, that she would be fine, that kids are resilient. But Lindsey was right, they shouldn't have to be. Jane was glad that she got it.

They conversed for a while longer, discussing the horrors of the foster system, Morgan Senior occasionally chiming in with gruff insistence that "something change", but otherwise remaining silent. He reminded Jane of Facundo.

When the game had come to an end, Jane had given Lindsey her email address for potential babysitting opportunities, and the family had packed their car-full of ballgame necessities away. Morgan Junior raced towards his parents with his small duffle bag dragging behind him, a big smile on his face despite his earlier devastation of not hitting the ball. Jane thought that his smile, though stretched over a much darker face, resembled his mother's.

The sun had begun to set, and as the orange glow seeped into the parking lot, Jane realized that her heart had lightened a great deal during the conversation in the stands. The family had been normal- vanilla, untouched by crime, and yet Jane had felt comfortable with them.

Her evening was almost nice, almost normal, but then her alarm bells rang.

The wind suddenly fell flat, and Jane's senses expanded to the breadth of the parking lot. In the far east end, an SUV was being loaded up with bags of bats and stacks of traffic cones. The man loading the materials was the coach. "Coach G", they'd said. The G stood for George, but the players' lisping voices had shouted "Coach G!" in their celebration at the end of the game. A little boy hopped around the car as the coach loaded up, the colorful backpack on his back jostling with each hop. Jane could hear the child talking excitedly to the coach and wondered if the child was his son. Something told her that he wasn't.

Suspicion won over anything else, and Jane pulled her truck out of the parking lot with the intention of following the man's SUV. A sticker on the back of it read, "I'm a coach, what's your superpower?" and the "o" in "coach" was designed to look like a baseball. She kept a close eye on the details of the vehicle, memorizing it in order to write it down later. She followed them all the way to a wildlife park, which was mostly just a nest of oaks and mesquite trees and a barred-off tank of water. A playground rested next to the parking lot. Jane drove around the other side of the parking lot as the SUV parked, driving as though she was heading towards the wooded area, and pulled up behind the brick building for restrooms. Once her headlights were off, she scampered behind the buildings, heart beating hard. There was no logical reason why someone would take a child to a park after hours, in the dark...not a good reason.

She wondered what effect she would have should she make herself known. Would Coach G harm her? Would he harm the child? Would he simply drive away to a more secure location?

These thoughts plagued her as she waited in the dark, praying that the man would emerge from the vehicle and simply take the child to push him on the swings. But he didn't.

She waited.

She waited longer.

The car sat in darkness, with no indication of what was happening inside.

After twenty-three minutes and fourteen seconds, the headlights came on. Jane leapt into her truck and waited until the SUV exited the parking lot before turning her truck on and leaving from the other exit.

She managed to catch up to the SUV with the baseball sticker on the back, hoping that her distance and the darkness would conceal the fact that she'd followed him before.

Coach G pulled up to a fast food restaurant, and Jane pulled in next to a dumpster in the lot to observe what he did. He ordered, pulled up to the window, exchanged cash for two cones of vanilla ice cream, and left.

Jane didn't have to follow them for much longer before the SUV stopped in front of a house and the boy with his tiny baseball pants and his little backpack climbed out of the vehicle. A woman wearing scrubs opened the screen door and stepped outside to greet him. Jane had the fleeting hope that the boy would run, screaming, up to his mother, and that she would be alerted to the situation and take charge. But no...the boy walked inside solemnly, despite his mother's attempts to embrace him, and the woman gave a friendly wave to Coach G before going inside herself. It was precisely what Jane had feared.

For many years, Jane had been told by counselors provided by her case worker that she may experience paranoia. She may fear that there are threats and danger where there is not. It occurred to her in her scenes over the years that she may be plotting the death of an innocent person.

She'd simply gotten more thorough.

Coach G was a sexual predator. She was almost positive that that was the case. Jane estimated that he was in his fifties, which meant that it was severely unlikely that this was his first victim. He'd more than likely begun his crimes years ago...there was no way this man didn't have a criminal record.

In the privacy of her home, she stripped off her costume, the one that had allowed her to make friends at baseball games like a normal woman, and threw on her boots. Wearing leather, working boots and a slip, she went out into the night to get into her shed and turn on the laptop she'd hooked internet up to deep in the confines of the insulated shed.

Once she was safely locked inside, she fired up the search engine and logged into the database she'd tried not to use in a while. An alert was sent out every time a police officer's pin number was used offsite, and the last thing she needed was someone looking into her harmless little search.

People found one another's license plate numbers all the time, but Jane was looking for more than that. She needed to know when and to whom this vehicle was registered, and once she discovered this, she could look for him in a directory of predators. There was no way he hadn't been busted for a sex crime before.

And there it was- the vehicle was not registered under anyone by the name of George, but rather, under the name of a California-based corporation. A corporation that hadn't been active in years.

Several names were listed as owners of the business, including a George Martin, and Jane quickly searched for all of them. Two of the men had separate businesses and social media accounts confirming their activity elsewhere, but George Martin and Phillip Caruthers had no activity anywhere, other than George's name showing up on the website for the little league regional teams, along with his email as the coach.

Jane took a moment to gather her thoughts and send up a prayer, one that was no doubt instantly rejected as soon as it reached God's ears. Then she typed in the last name.

Phillip Caruthers appeared on the sex offender registry, clear as day. He was first registered as a child molester nearly two decades prior, but had no offenses extending past that. Jane sincerely doubted that this was due to a change in character, and more likely due to a change in identity.

Researching his alias, George Martin, a bit more, Jane became grimly satisfied in her resolution to put research on her father's case on hold until she'd handled "Coach G". She could barely stomach the fact that she hadn't taken action in the park, regardless of how risky it was to do so, there was no way she was wasting another moment.

Cundo threw a sports coat over his western shirt and descended from his loft with hesitation. He wasn't terribly keen on participating in the rowdier nights at The Red Light, but it didn't look good if the owner didn't make an appearance. Frank had hired an assistant for the cook and a few temporary waiters and waitresses for the new events he'd insisted on. Reluctantly, he'd allowed Frank to take the reins on gathering interest in the bar, inviting local bands and artists to come by on Friday nights and attract a larger variety of customers. The music that came in was adequate, any lack of skill swallowed up in an eclectic aesthetic and deliberate idiosyncrasies. Some of them were bluegrass hipsters in straw hats, some were almost jazz bands, but not quite. Some were just college students looking for a place to begin. Frank was skeptical about letting almost anyone play, but Cundo didn't feel like it was a big deal. The kids needed experience, and a bar built into a library couldn't be picky about style.

There were far more customers on Friday nights than there were when Cundo had first opened the bar. Before, there were mostly locals, but now tourists came in from off the beaten path to see the unusual theme of the bar, stranded in the middle of a desert town, hosting odd assortments of music and art.

Tonight, Cundo would utilize all the liquor at his disposal and fend off his growing hunger for the blood of Phillip Caruthers. He simply couldn't continue to think this way, he needed to stay on top of his plan.

As he stepped down into the rustic interior of his bar, his buddies greeted him.

"Hey!" Diego exclaimed, loosening his hold on a redheaded girl that seemed to be using him as a means to stay afloat in invisible water.

"Hey."

"I thought I'd have to drag you down here," quipped Til, who was cozied up to a less enthusiastic looking woman holding both their beers.

"You almost did. I really didn't want to come down when I saw the crowd."

The men laughed good-naturedly, but Cundo's aversions to crowd and noise stemmed back to his PTSD from his service, and there was darkness within the inside joke.

The bar was packed with dusty old desert men and fresh young people who looked like they'd traveled far. From between his curtains upstairs, he'd seen cars that weren't trucks filing into the parking lot. It was always a shock to see a packed night, but tonight was a little different, perhaps a result of the particular choice in music this evening. A more successful, but still new group of college students who had returned home for the summer to make music- the lead singer was a young woman with bright pink cowboy boots who reminded Cundo of Jane. He tried to keep his eyes off her shoes in order to avoid the memory of Jane's spiked heels.

"I don't think she's seeing anybody," Til said slyly, sidling up to Cundo as he watched the band.

"I'm not even remotely interested in her, she's a child," Cundo replied instantly with his usual, chafed tone.

"No way, college girls are the perfect age- they have experience and they're adults but they're still young enough to be stupid with you."

Till laughed at his own joke, and to his side, Cundo saw his date catch his comment and roll her eyes. Tonight seemed to be one of those nights- people on edge, something unnameable wrong. Or perhaps that was simply the sensation Cundo received when he was unlucky enough to find himself in a busy place.

The music grew to a crescendo, and Cundo watched as the young woman in front of the microphone closed her eyes as if in ecstasy over the notes. While watching her, he decided that she looked nothing like Jane after all. Though Jane appeared young at first glance, she held none of the authentic innocence and freshness of this singer. Her youth looked opaque, a hard, smooth shell covering something more sinister inside.

Or perhaps that was simply the spite over her insult talking.

"Cundo," Diego interrupted his thoughts. "If you want to go chill somewhere, I can handle things with Frank."

Diego could always sense when something was off with his friend- several years of service together had solidified an almost telepathic bond. Cundo nodded appreciatively at Diego and then made a sudden, heart-thumping decision.

"Yeah, I'm going out for a bit...clear my head...if anyone asks, I'm here, though."

He looked hard at Diego, and the man searched his face, then nodded. He seemed to understand and blessedly asked no questions.

Pulling off his sports coat and retrieving a case from his office, he escaped through the back entrance.

Jane enjoyed every element of the scene, including things that took a great deal of time and patience. But tonight, Jane was eager to complete the scene and be done with it.

It's not that she'd never killed a child molester before- she had. She'd even stalked and hunted one for months, finding out every repulsive morsel of his deeds before ending him. But tonight, she desperately wanted this man's life to end and to move on from it quickly. She felt uncharacteristic guilt over not having listened to her instincts and accosting him in the park before he could hurt the little t-ball player. Usually, she didn't feel guilty knowing that her prey would never be able to do anything like it again, but she wished this man never existed- she wished Phillip Caruthers, or George Martin, or whoever he was, hadn't ever been born.

Although he deserved a slow and painful death, his would have to look like a suicide. It was risky enough killing someone who had ties in the community. She couldn't afford for anything to be out of place. She had all of her extra materials- sterilized and taken from her home without a trace- just in case he didn't have what she needed. Worst case scenario, he would make things messy and she would have to use her Glock 40...and then find out how to make it look like he owned a Glock 40.

She hoped that once she set up her evidence, no one would feel inclined to look too deeply into his death. Something dark and vengeful in humans prevented them from feeling sympathetic to the death of a sex offender.

She carefully tucked her hair into a slicked-back braid on top of her head, removing any stray hairs from her person that could be dropped at the scene. Her hands of course were possessed of thin, nylon gloves (couldn't leave any evidence on the body if he happened to be allergic to latex), and her t-shirt clad elbows and cargo-pant-covered knees additionally protected by volleyball pads. She'd learned her lesson where protection was concerned. One never knew when they were going to need to jump from a window or run on difficult terrain, and blood at the scene and incriminating injuries were not a slip-up Jane intended to be brought down by.

With her boots on, gun at her hip, an extra clip holstered, and her backpack filled with the necessities, she set up a light in her bedroom and dropped the needle on a record turning on her turntable. If she turned up the volume loud enough, it would help any passerbys confirm that she is in fact here, and leave an excuse as to why she hadn't answered the door. One can never be too careful.

"I met a girl a month ago…"

She turned the volume up and turned on the automatic setting to reset the needle once the album was completed.

"I thought that she would love me so…"

Jane secured every entrance to the house and retrieved her bicycle.

"But in time I realized…"

She mapped out the path to Coach G's house in her mind, the one she'd mapped out on paper again and again to memorize the fastest route. Once she was confident that she needed nothing more from her father's cabin, she took off.

"She had a pair of roving eyes."

Coach G's house, or rather, Phillip Caruther's house, had a neat and homey facade, but the obvious signs of bachelorhood existed. A couple plastic chairs on the front porch and nothing adorning the fence or front yard. Jane wondered if he ever brought any of his victims home. Was it with their parents' permission? Did they have any suspicions? They couldn't possibly. Jane considered for a moment the fact that she'd never allow any child of her own to be in the presence of someone she hadn't thoroughly vetted ahead of time. Indeed, there was no one left alive that she already knew she could trust, save a couple previous foster parents.

As Jane deftly disappeared into the wooded area to the side of the house, she tried to shake herself free of that last, disturbing thought. The last thing she should be doing right now was allowing herself to consider for the first time what her life would be like with children. She couldn't even consider it, it wasn't something she could afford. At any moment, the world could be ripped out from under her and she could be charged with murder of one of her victims. And there was no way she could stop...nothing would ever satiate her desire to cleanse the earth of the vile predators that preyed on the weak. Nothing could make her stop, she knew that she would simply do it until she was caught. She would only attempt to escape the notice of the authorities so that she could do as much as she could for the betterment of society until that inevitable day.

She'd never throw a child into the fray the way she had been in her youth- she knew too much about how evil the world could be to a kid, never mind how evil one could be to the offspring of a murderer. And that's what she was, no matter how she spinned her motives.

In the wooded area, she was invisible, and she lifted her lightweight bike off the ground so that it didn't make a noise among the branches on the ground. She stepped nimbly, her sharp eyesight catching all the possible obstacles on the ground. Once she'd traversed the trees parallel to the house, and found herself behind it, she propped her bike up against a tree and tightened the straps of her backpack.

One of the essential elements of a scene was not moving until you had a plan. When you find a safe place, stay there for as long as you can. The trees were safe, and Jane could not move until she figured out an entrance plan. For the past couple of weeks, Jane had been tracking "Coach G's" schedule, and she knew that Friday evenings were early endings to practice, and he would come home just after the sun went down, unless he had plans to prey on someone. One odd development was noticing that Coach G shared a schedule with someone else that Jane had searched for information on- Facundo "Del Sur" Locklear.

Jane had run into Cundo during her hunting, and while pleasantries were exchanged, she could tell that he wasn't eager to communicate with her. What did she expect? This was the desired outcome- no interference from random people. So why did she feel as if she missed their repartee...

She couldn't let Facundo Locklear into her mind at this moment- it was imperative that every second was spent with a clear mind and complete focus.

She needed to get into the house. She would take Coach G by surprise when he entered the home, and if he brought a guest, they would have to be a casualty. Perhaps his guest could "stumble upon incriminating evidence, and he would have no choice but to shoot them." Jane prayed that if someone were to arrive with her target, they were not a child, but another adult, preferably one with a criminal record.

From the trees, Jane spied a screened window that appeared to be open. It wasn't uncommon for frugal southerners to leave un-air-conditioned houses open to the night air to let the heat out when they weren't home, and simply draw the shades during the day. If Phillip Caruthers had changed his identity before, he more than likely didn't have the money to spend on climate control in his home.

Jane acted swiftly, moving under the moonlight to reach the window quickly. Her hair- still wet, was black and matted enough not to reveal her signature sheen in the darkness. Her black clothes encased her body in shadows.

Using her knife, she pried the edge of the window screen up, and was satisfied when it popped out, leaving no outstanding scratches on the already rusticated frame. Heaving herself up onto the high window ledge, supporting herself on padded knees, she propelled herself into what appeared to be a bedroom and landed on her hands and knees. Her backpack jostled on her back, but didn't throw her off balance. She left the screen hanging, not popped back into the frame to make for a one-way entrance and exit- easier to erase evidence from one space than from two.

Time to go to work.

It was only fifteen minutes- her window had been too close, she would have to work on that, though not bad for a meager two weeks of investigation. Fifteen minutes between her falling into his bedroom and keys jingling in the door. Fifteen minutes to locate his office area, complete with computer, find the most likely areas for him to hide souvenirs from previous victims, and to wrap a scarf around her head that concealed her identity.

Fifteen minutes, and then he was in the house.

In the darkness, Jane chose the place where the climax of the scene would begin- around the corner from the kitchen in the shadows of the hallway.

"Coach G's" heavy footsteps announced his arrival, and she heard him drop his bag onto a kitchen chair, and stop to do something on his phone, the digital sounds of clicking and scrolling notifying her of his location. Finally, he relieved himself of his keys and made his way to the kitchen.

It was time.

Click.

Satisfying, iconic. Anyone would know what that signature sound meant. The man that had passed her and paused in the hallway was no exception. His hands were empty, and his loose t-shirt and basketball shorts could conceal no potential weapon. Though his stature was larger than hers, he was portly and slow, his gate lazy and his hands weak and soft with a lack of activity. Jane didn't bike, run, and box just to be beaten by a cowardly, unathletic child molester. Especially not when she was armed.

Coach G was stopped, and Jane's heart pounded as she waited for him to turn around. This moment was crucial- it could go any way. If his instincts took over and he fled or fought back, it could get messy. Luckily for her, the coach seemed to be familiar with the tough spot he was in.

He turned slowly, and she almost flinched at his face. She didn't want to see him up close, his proclivities disgusted her. She felt sick and filthy just looking at him. His eyes were wide, but his hands were steady as he raised them. His forehead was already perspiring.

Good.

"Where do you keep your souvenirs?" she asked, her voice only slightly muffled by the tightly-wound scarf.

Coach G's eyes flickered for a moment.

"I keep my money in my safe. I don't know what you want, but I'll do-"

"You know what I'm talking about, take me to your souvenirs," Jane's voice had dropped into the black, emotionless chill that she spoke in when she was in the scene. The way actors were on stage- consumed by their character, unable to remove themselves from it, unaffected by biological human needs. Jane was like that in the scene- her impatience didn't show, and that made her prey even more nervous.

Coach G's pale gaze flickered between the barrel of the gun and Jane's petite stature. She almost seethed, but her focus was too razor-sharp to waver.

"I know you have some. Your kind always has them- bring me to the things you take from the kids you molest."

She'd seen her prey do it plenty of times before, but a nasty gratification germinated in her empty chest when his face paled further, and his mouth drew down and open in horror.

That's right, she thought. You're already dead.

"I'll let you live," she lied. "If you show me your souvenirs."

"Why-why would you want-"

"Move."

The command, along with the promise of life, spurred him forward, and he intelligently kept his hands on the back of his sparsely-covered scalp. Jane's stomach unclenched once he was turned around, but she hardly noticed- she was too far into the scene.

In his bedroom, Coach G used one hand, the other on his head, to remove a box from the top shelf of his closet. It was a simple, unassuming shoe box, but Jane already felt uneasy about it- the black ice running through her crystallizing at the thought of what this man possessed.

Opening it, slowly as instructed, Jane kept her gun on the coach, and her eyes ran over the contents of the box. This was all she needed. All she really needed was for it to be open, and she certainly didn't want to handle any of the materials- so precious and yet so corrupted. There was a couple of bracelets with colorful string and beads, a hand-made card of construction paper, a baseball, and to her disgust, a set of plastic keys- the kind that teething babies chew on.

"Pick your favorite," she said in a low voice, some of that fire of her fury breaking through the ice. The coach didn't bother asking what she meant, he reached inside and picked up the baseball. She noticed a name written in permanent marker on the side.

"Let's go."

She prodded him in the back with her gun, her Glock poking him in the back as he kept his hands above his head, one hand clenched around the baseball. Once they entered his office, she urged him to once again use one hand to turn on the computer, and watched carefully, standing out of the way of the laptop's camera. She barked out instructions, and watched with barely-concealed aversion as he pulled up downloaded videos...child pornography. No matter how many times she saw it pulled up by one of her prey, she would never be able to control the bile that rose in her throat.

Now for the finishing touch on the canvas.

"You want me to what?"

They were back in his bedroom, and she'd handed him a notepad and pen from his desk.

"Write their names."

"No," he said firmly, only a slight tremble giving him away.

"Yes," she replied. "Don't you want to live?"

"You're going to kill me anyway," he whimpered, and to her horror, tears began to trickle from his swollen eyelids. She sneered.

"If my plan was to kill you, I wouldn't have bothered to conceal my identity."

His eyebrows pulled together in confusion.

"What do you want from me, then? I told you, I have money, I can pay you, whoever is paying you, I can give you twice-"

"Shut the fuck up," her ice cracked, and she clutched her gun hard, her arm starting to get tired. "I don't want your money, and you can't sway me. Now write the fucking names."

Coach G's Adam's apple worked up and down and he began to shakily scrawl away at the paper. She watched him list one after another, and by the time he was done, eleven names were on the paper.

"You have to understand, it's not something I can control, it's not like I want to-"

"Now apologize."

"I'm...I'm sorry."

"Not to me, you vile, cowardly, inconsequential stain," she spat out, each word causing him to flinch. "To them." She nodded down at the paper.

Understanding dawned on his face, and he swallowed his sobs as he scrawled out a tearful apology. She struggled to read it upside-down, but she could make out some more of his excuses on the paper. She refrained from hitting him.

Leaving the notepad and pen on his side table, Jane encouraged him to walk ahead of her, pushing him towards the guest bedroom. There, hanging from the ceiling fan, was a noose.

Coach G whipped around and tried to squeeze between Jane and the doorframe to escape, but she shoved the barrel of her gun under his chin. He stopped in his tracks, breathing heavily, not making a move to turn back. He'd been cooperative up until now, and Jane had wondered when his instincts would get the better of him.

"Don't make things messy," she whispered. "Or I won't have a reason to make things fast and easy for you."

This didn't seem to calm the man down, but instead caused him to choke out a panicked cry.

"You said-"

"Don't be any more pathetic than you already are. Get on the chair."

Coach G looked around frantically, but walked with shaking legs to the chair and climbed onto it under the noose as instructed. She'd learned that if she kept a calm countenance, her prey's instincts would cause them to automatically do as told or simply freeze up, rather than flee or fight back. Right now, as if hypnotized, the man did as he was told at gunpoint, his frantically-moving eyes finding nothing helpful.

"Put your head in the noose."

He did it.

"Close your eyes."

He did.

Something made her want to memorize this man's face at that moment. She wanted him to be terrified. She wanted to remember the power she had in this moment forever. She always wanted to remember- she couldn't afford to take souvenirs like the animals she hunted, and she didn't truly want to, but she wanted to remind herself that she was a predator amongst predators, at the apex of the food chain, the one that those beneath her had to answer to for upsetting the balance.

She wanted to remember this feeling.

She unwound her scarf and told him to open his eyes.

He did.

She wasn't sure what he saw, but her naked face did something to the man, and as he scrambled in his precariously-balanced position on the chair, it toppled over, and he fell, pulling the noose taut. Jane stepped back unhurriedly and watched as his hands shot up to claw at the noose, but he was a few inches shy of gaining traction on the floor, and he'd knocked the chair too far to use its side. The ceiling fan made a horrific noise as his weight strained it, the rope moving with the force of his scrambling and pushing the blades around in a sad, slow mockery of his plight. Jane was sure that the ceiling fan would collapse with all his movement, but as he stared at her in desperation, eyes bulging, face puffing, tongue protruding, fingers desperately attempting to get between his skin and the coarse rope around his neck, she could tell that he would expire before the ceiling fan did. His panic was causing him to use oxygen more quickly, and as he fought to pull a breath in, Jane let a slow, exhausted smile creep across her face. She'd done it. She'd rid the earth of this diseased animal- this vermin that would infect anyone he touched with trauma and pain. He was going to disappear. She'd done it.

Finally, his widened eyes, red with busted capillaries, went empty, and his hands fell slack to his sides. The toes of his sneakers dipped towards the floor, but didn't quite touch. The ceiling creaked, but remained whole as she tentatively stepped forward and studied him. His pupils were wide despite the light and remained so even as she stared into them. Jane pulled a compact mirror from her pocket and held it under his nose. No cloud of breath vapor. In one last test, she put two fingers to his corroded artery and breathed a heavy sigh of satisfaction when she realized that his pulse had stopped completely.

Stepping back to study her handiwork, she gave one last nod before retrieving his notepad from his bedroom and setting it on the table beside the guest bed. She read the note, then paused and reread it.

"I'm sorry for all the people I hurt, the kids, and the people they love. I'm sorry, mom, I'm sorry about my brother. I didn't mean to hit him so hard, I just couldn't stop myself when I got angry. I get angry so fast, I can hide it, but I can't always, I don't really want to hurt anyone. I'm sorry, Maria, I never meant to hurt you or your son, I'm so sorry. You were good to me."

It was a frantic, stream of consciousness series of thoughts, probably writing as his sins occurred to him. She wondered briefly who Maria was and if she and her son needed reparations, but decided that Maria would be just fine once she'd caught wind of the death of Phillip Caruthers.

Jane left the note on the table and returned to holster her weapon, gather her things, and search the house for any loose ends before ghosting back out of the bedroom window.

Her job here was done.

It had taken a good forty-five minutes of U-turns and gut-wrenching pep talks to get Cundo to Phillip Caruther's driveway. He didn't really want to kill anyone, not after his years in the service, but there wasn't any reason not to. Logically, his imprisonment wouldn't affect anyone, and he knew that his soul was already damned. Nothing else incentivized his good behavior. He always thought that if he'd committed to this decision, that he would be hard, stoic, and immovable. Instead, he sobbed in the cabin of his truck.

You could always turn him in.

No. He needed to die, and Cundo was going to deliver that necessity tonight, before he lost his nerve.

Pulling up along the road past the driveway, Cundo made his way along the treeline to the house, following the light gleaming from a window in the back. Gun in hand, he wondered if he should even attempt to make it look like a home invasion, or if that would be necessary. It might buy him a little time if he wanted to tie up loose ends.

As Cundo pondered this, his legs growing stiff, his eyes and ears growing hot, his hands shaking and the barrel of the gun twitching this way and that, he noticed a shape flicker across the ground. A shadow. Him.

Cundo slowed and crept closer to the house, using the shadows against the walls as cover. He rounded the corner to the back of the wood-slatted house, the ground at its base dry and uncovered by flower beds or drainage beds of rock.

Cundo darted from the shadows of the house to the shadows of a nearby shed when he realized that he couldn't be seen through the windows that were covered in blinds. From his hiding place beside the shed, gun drawn, muscles coiled and ready to confront the shadow, he could see the window with the light on. The shadow moved closer to the window, and he saw its definition more clearly.

This was not his intended target, this shadow did not belong to Phillip Caruthers. This shadow was slender and feminine. He'd checked- Caruthers didn't have any plans tonight. He'd been stalking the man for months each week, and not once had a woman ever entered his home, and for good reason- the man simply didn't want one there.

But this was unmistakably the shadow of a grown woman. Cundo watched with rapt attention as the shadow stood poised before the window with its thin curtains drawn. As the shadow turned slightly, he saw her hair piled high on her head, falling away from her and down her back in a sleek formation. Cundo felt his heart nearly restart. His breath left his body on a curse, and he dropped his gun to his side.

He wasn't one to play into superstition, it was hard enough for him to keep a grasp on his faith. But this shadow appeared to belong to none other than Maria Locklear- his beautiful mother. Her familiar shape was framed by the window, her signature braid, simple and thickly wound, was probably what he could see on the back of her head. Despite his utter disbelief in the supernatural, Cundo felt that without a doubt, the woman standing at the window was his mother.

He could practically hear her voice telling him not to come closer to the house.

Her shadow wavered.

Don't come closer, Cundo.

You don't need to do this.

The shadow moved, and he desperately wished she would part the curtains and show him the visage of his mother's spirit. Even with the veil of life and death between them, this was a moment that would never arrive for him again. He had wished for one more moment with his mother for years, sobbing into his pillow at night at the memory of her demise from teenagerhood well into his life as a man. And before him, she stood, a mere shadow.

His soul is damned.

Cundo could feel it in his bones. His mother never would have said something like that in life, but the phantom in the window seemed to say it to him. Don't worry, she seemed to say. He won't escape this life without paying his due.

He opened and closed his mouth, pulling air into his lungs and forcing himself to stay rooted to the spot, his eyes filling with tears as he simply nodded to his mother's shadow, feeling the weight of twenty years lift from his sore shoulders.

His mother, the woman that had unburdened him at every opportunity, his only protector, was taking this from him, removing the responsibility from his person and taking it upon herself in spirit. He could simply feel it.

Cundo fell to his knees in the dry earth beside the shed and wept silently, feeling a relief, painful in its power, descended over him as he realized for the first time that he was no longer responsible for making Phillip Caruthers pay. He no longer needed to. He simply no longer needed to.

CHAPTER 11

Harpy Eagle, Harpia harpyja

Facundo Locklear laid back on his sofa with his beer, feeling free of gravity. He stared up at the ceiling of his loft and savored the sensation of the cool, worn leather at his back, a sensation he couldn't feel if he were around anyone other than his closest friends. Only Diego, Til, and Frank were allowed to see him so casually adorned, shirtless and in basketball shorts. Cundo would be concerned about anyone else seeing the scars crawling up his right thigh to his chest, back, shoulder, and face.

But on this Sunday afternoon, Cundo felt particularly generous with his comfortability, and bestowed it upon his friends without a care. They weren't certain of why he was in such a good mood, but they weren't going to ask for fear of ruining it. They simply continued to play pool on Cundo's personal felt in his loft, emptying one beer after another and enjoying the air conditioning.

It had only taken two days for word to spread about the town, and two days after that for it to make it to the news.

Phillip Caruthers had committed suicide.

Or rather, George Martin had. But the people of Zemsta were corrected once investigators released his true identity to the media.

Of all the possible outcomes, Cundo never considered that the man would do his dirty work for him, but he supposed that was a relief after discovering why he did it. After hearing about the list of children he'd assaulted in his suicide note, Cundo had at first been furious at the cowardice, wishing that he'd turned him in when he had the chance, knowing how sex offenders fair in prison. However, when it was revealed in a community-wide outrage that his most recent victims had been t-ball players that he'd been in the process of grooming and molesting when he took his life, Cundo realized that it was for the best that he'd been taken out of commission before he had a chance to hurt anyone else or escape the authorities and flee to another town of potential victims.

Cundo had always been of the firm belief that child molesters were deserving of the harshest possible punishments known to humankind. There was no excuse for hurting a child; even the most devout religious zealots who believed in complete judgement after life, or the most zen of all pacifists, felt a bloodlust where the safety of children were concerned. At the end of the day, they were all animals, and their instincts to protect their young would win out.

Since news of Caruthers's death had reached his ears, Cundo had felt one difficult emotion after the next. He was furious, then he was gleeful. He was coldly terrified, wondering how his mother's spirit had played into it. He was concerned about people opening up his mother's murder case, and his identity being aired out for the town to see.

Finally, he'd settled on grim satisfaction, and he was simply enjoying the aftermath of the community discovering the man's betrayal, and the complete defamation of "Coach G" that followed. Today, Cundo merely cracked open one beer after another, sending all of his concerns sky high- just as his mother wanted.

"Hey, I gotta tell you something," Diego said from the pool table, his also unabashedly shirtless self looking a little more sheepish than was characteristic.

"Yeah?" Cundo was unconcerned with anything his friend could present to him.

"I saw Jane the other day."

Perhaps not that unconcerned.

"Oh yeah?"

"Yeah...I ran into her in town, we got to talking. I remembered how you said that date didn't go well and you didn't care..."

Cundo already knew where Diego's speech was heading. His beautiful friend had never been able to keep his heavy-lashed green eyes off of anyone of the female sex, and they seemed to have the same trouble.

"What did she say?" Cundo asked, not bothering to inquire as to whether or not Diego had asked Jane on a date, or for her phone number, or for her to simply strip naked and dance with him in the town square. She would undoubtedly have said yes to any of them.

"She said yes." Precisely.

"Yeah, I don't care. No big deal, man."

"Are you sure?" Diego seemed more hesitant than Cundo had ever seen him. His cool confidence had waned, and perhaps it was because he'd never picked up Cundo's scraps before. Cundo hadn't been on a real date with a woman that could stick around to meet Diego in years. The situation was usually the other way around, and women would flirt or even attempt to seduce the pretty man's disfigured friend to get back at him for losing interest in her.

"Yeah, I don't care," he repeated, keeping his eyes on his ceiling and hoping that what he said was true.

Diego and Til's conversation picked back up, and Cundo listened to the pool balls clack together and the men's beers hiss upon opening. He didn't care. It was true, he didn't care. He didn't have to care about anything anymore- his troubles were over, his demons slain.

Jane fidgeted in the passenger seat, a trait that was not typical to her character. She never fidgeted, but she felt on edge in Diego's car. Not that Diego made her uncomfortable, but the entire scenario was unfamiliar to her.

She wasn't sure why she'd said yes to the man's sly come-on in the middle of the department store. She didn't fawn over pretty men like other women, and she had no intention of hurting him, as something about his character felt comfortable and safe. But something in the back of her mind pulled out a picture of Cundo and told her to grasp this opportunity.

Why.

She was still wondering as they pulled out of the restaurant parking lot. Dinner had been nice, uneventful, and she'd managed to pull it off without saying anything off-color or sending any red flags up. Without an objective, she wasn't sure what to say or do. She supposed she could behave the way one would do if they were sexually interested in someone, but she wasn't sure if she wanted him to believe that about her. After all, she wasn't. Despite his obviously stunning physique, the wavy hair that always looked perfectly tousled, and the dimple to the right of his crooked smile, she simply couldn't muster up enough interest in him to challenge her modus operandi of using and losing men- using them for information and losing them when she was done with a scene.

Even now, looking at the muscles in his bicep flex as he turned his steering wheel, she couldn't associate him with any sexual feelings. Every time her mind seemed to inch in that direction, a wave of memories of abuse would crash over her, and memories of teenage boys' sweaty, fumbling hands in locker rooms and youthful bedrooms would swell in her throat, and she would instantly forget the sensation of want. She supposed that she could attempt to override the feelings and take a risk now that she'd made a bit more headway with her father's case- perhaps it would provide a bit more clarity of mind. And if she were to try to be a normal woman for once, she could do much worse than the poster boy for the Marine Corps sitting beside her.

But as her eyes roamed over Diego's thickly muscled, denim-clad thighs and the veined hands that gripped the steering wheel, she felt something rise up. She prepared for the onslaught of memories and PTSS, but instead, a vision of Facundo Locklear appeared in her mind's eye, and she watched in shock as the man next to her transformed into the man she'd sat beside in a truck mere weeks ago. Facundo had worn a button-down shirt, too, the sleeves rolled up over taut forearms that led down to fine hands with long fingers. She saw his hair- black and thick, shiny, curling around his ears and over the ruined side of his face. The scars over his brow and cheekbone that sunk his eye and curled the lips that she wanted to outline with her fingertips.

Jane physically shook her head, knocking the thoughts out of her head quickly. Undoubtedly, she was possessed with these thoughts due to the adrenaline and dopamine running through her after her recent scene. She always had strange thoughts and notions post-kill. It was only natural, she told herself.

"What are you thinking about over there?" Diego suddenly asked, causing Jane to consider how obvious her thoughts might be.

"Just thinking about how nice you look tonight," she answered smoothly, shooting him a suggestive smile when he looked over at her. He didn't respond and she wondered if that was the right answer.

She'd been so caught up in her thoughts that she hadn't noticed where they'd been heading. If she was in a scene right now, she more than likely would already be dead, she thought, kicking herself mentally.

Diego pulled his sleek, low pick-up into a parking spot in front of The Red Light, and parked.

"Okay, look. I know you probably think I'm crazy for coming here, but this is one of the few bars in town where I would actually take a woman."

Jane mused on that, wondering how Diego would take it if he knew the seedy places she'd gone to kill men far worse than he'd ever seen.

"Besides, Cundo isn't working here tonight, he's out," Diego promised. At that, her stomach flipped, and not in a pleasant way. She wasn't sure why, but she felt disappointed to hear that the Cundo wasn't yards away inside like she'd for some reason hoped. Her head was playing tricks on her this evening.

Diego opened her car door like a gentleman and helped her down, even though his car was nothing like Cundo's, which required him to actually pick her up out of the truck. The man was a beast.

Diego took her hand, causing her to jump a bit, thankfully unnoticed by him, and led her inside.

To her surprise, a band was playing- a woman stood in front of a small band in the corner of the bar, one unoccupied by books, wearing pink cowboy boots. Jane admired them, wondering where she could obtain a pair for herself. She warbled out a tune in that indie-feminine way that was popular and rocked her body to the music her band made behind her with guitars, drums, and for some reason, a banjo. Jane cocked her head to listen, imagining that if they had a few more years of practice, they'd probably be rather talented.

Diego led her to a high table with bar chairs where Cundo's friend, Til, was already seated with a blonde hanging on his arm. The blonde caught sight of Diego and immediately threw her arms around Til's shoulders, smiling fawningly up at him. Til seemed unaware of the motivation behind her sudden attention- that or unconcerned.

"Hey, man, how's it going?" Til said excitedly, doing the half man-hug with Diego, who charmingly didn't let go of Jane's hand through the exchange.

"Good; Jane and I just got back from dinner."

Til frowned down at their hands, and Jane wondered what could possibly bring on a negative reaction in the seemingly ever-chipper man. Jane considered that Cundo may have told him what she'd said to him after their date. For some reason, that gave her a sick feeling. *Since when do I give a shit what a man thinks of my character...*

"Cool," he responded without emotion, turning back to his blonde and his beer.

Diego shot Jane an apologetic look and helped her on to a bar chair.

"I'll be right back, what do you want to drink?"

"A shirley temple," she answered automatically, and Diego barked out a surprised laugh and left her to retrieve their drinks.

Not one to typically be concerned with the inner thoughts of someone she wasn't running from or trying to kill, Jane ignored Til and the handsy blonde, and glued her eyes to the band. As the cowgirl boot-bearing girl started up a new song, Jane saw movement out of the corner of her eye, and the hair on the back of her neck pricked up. She searched with her gaze without turning her head, and saw a tall, broad figure looming over the crowd from the terrace of the loft.

Abandoning self-preservation, she turned completely to face the phantom leaning on the railing, unnoticed by the crowd.

He was staring at her, scarred and unscarred sides both in full view. His hair was tousled and his t-shirt was tight over his massive chest and shoulders. He looked almost inhuman. He was beautiful.

Jane's skin felt taut over her body, and she shuddered in a breath, watching Cundo continue to be immobile. She forced her gaze back to the band and tried not to turn back, wondering what he thought of her this evening; it felt as if he could see through her like an Antarctic icefish, her organs on display. She suddenly felt exposed in her sundress, the pink, floral design feeling unattractively ironic compared to the filth in her soul that it seemed Cundo could see. Could he tell that she'd killed not once, but twice recently?

She was usually in complete control of her body, but she couldn't control her arms as she crossed them to cover herself. She'd allowed more of her cleavage than usual to be on display, not knowing what character to dress for when she was supposed to be herself on a date. But under Cundo's scrutiny, everything she had on felt ridiculous.

Diego finally returned with their drinks, and Jane glanced up to the loft, noticing that Cundo had disappeared.

"No one carted you off while I was gone, huh?" Diego asked playfully, leaning into her chair from where he stood. Jane felt no desire to lean back, nor did she find the desire to lean away, and without a motive to behave in a specific way, she simply sat. She probably looked like a doll, stiff and unmoving, but she didn't really care.

"I don't think anyone would cart me off in here. Only you're brave enough to risk Cundo's wrath after I upset him. Isn't there some kind of policy amongst 'bros'?" she said laughingly, but Diego's eyebrows pulled together and he made a strange face.

"What do you mean? How did you upset him?"

"Oh, I figured y'all would have discussed that..." she trailed off and looked at Til, who had blatantly been listening in on their conversation, and appeared to know exactly what she meant.

"No?" Diego said hesitantly, and Jane moved in quickly, knowing that regardless of her lack of motive, she didn't want anyone to know what she said to Cundo. She wasn't sure why, but she wanted to erase that particular comment, regardless of why she made it.

"I said something stupid," she answered quickly. "It doesn't matter."

"It mattered to him," Til muttered around his beer from the other side of the bar table. Diego looked between Til and Jane, and Jane felt an alien sensation rise up to her cheeks- shame. She didn't want Cundo to be upset by what she said, but she couldn't afford his attention. She also couldn't afford to have an internal conflict over the necessities of the scene. This was her biggest scene yet; her plot to uncover and destroy her father's murderer was the most important thing she'd ever devised, and she couldn't allow a random man to distract her when she'd never allowed one to distract her before.

"Let's dance," Jane chimed in suddenly, grabbing Diego and dragging him to the small crowd of people that were moving in synchronization to the music in front of the band. Diego looked like he wanted to ask about her comment again, so Jane pulled him close and wrapped her arms around his neck.

What the hell am I doing? She didn't know how to dance.

Diego found her hips and gripped the skirt of her dress lightly, pulling her against him. His nearness would have had her hyperventilating years ago, but she'd grown, and without the potential threat of the prey she was usually seducing in some fashion, she felt no alarm bells pressed against him.

He simply wasn't enticing.

Despite the hard body she was pressed against, Jane had to fight to keep her eyes from wandering up to the loft to search for the phantom that wouldn't stop haunting her. Attempting to roll her body the way she'd seen people do with dance partners, she did her best to distract Diego and keep him from asking questions, but her skills were not substantial enough to make that happen.

"I don't want to get between you and Cundo if the two of you are having some kind of disagreement," he said firmly. Jane caught a glimpse of the ex-marine in his seriousness, and she wondered what kind of things he and Cundo had witnessed together.

"We're not," she whispered back sweetly, running her hands down his biceps. "It wasn't a big deal, we went on one date, and we just didn't click."

"It doesn't seem that simple."

"Like I said, it wasn't a big-"

"Did you go on a date with him to get to me?"

Jane looked up at him and almost laughed when she realized that he was dead serious.

"What?!"

"Girls have done that before," he replied, studying her. "That's not fair to him, and I would just appreciate the truth."

Jane stifled a giggle and responded, "I can honestly say that seeing you had not occurred to me at any point during our extremely brief courtship."

Diego searched her face for a moment and seemed satisfied with her answer. He took her hand and twirled her around, pulling her back to him before flinging her back out. She giggled at the motion and considered that if dancing with men always included such things, it might actually be fun.

The pink cowgirl boot girl hit a crescendo and held onto a powerful note, her band rattling excitedly on their instruments until the very end. Diego spun her around and around, holding her hand high above her head. Her skirt billowed around her, lifting up to reveal the lightweight petticoat she sported underneath. She laughed out loud in genuine glee and collapsed against Diego when the music came to a stop. Leaning back into him, she smiled at the sound of him laughing, allowing herself the enjoyment of three minutes of normalcy.

Then she saw him.

He was leaning against their table, whiskey tumbler in hand, and Til was talking to him but keeping his eyes on her. The smile fell off her face.

She wanted Cundo's attention, she realized with a start. She wanted his mind on her, for him to need to talk to her, for his obsidian eyes to follow her every move. Why she wanted to be seen when it was the most dangerous thing for her, she couldn't possibly know.

Diego loosened his hold on her and began to propel her to the table. She moved automatically but went slowly, stalling their inevitable proximity to one another. What would she say? How should she act?

You can't afford for him to want you.

The thought was painful but correct. It was almost a relief to have a goal in her interactions. Jane snaked an arm around Diego's waist and fell in step with him. Perhaps Cundo's gaze would stray if she gave him something he didn't want to watch.

"Evening, boys," Diego drawled. Cundo's gaze dipped to where Diego's hand still rested on her hip, but the black depths of his eyes revealed nothing.

"Evening," Cundo's deep voice responded. Jane practically felt his vibrato dance across her skin.

She backed up against Diego, pulling the hand on her hip all the way around her waist and looked off at the band casually, as if this closeness was something she allowed on a regular basis. Diego played along and grabbed his beer, striking up a conversation with Til's date about her job. She brightened immeasurably when Diego acknowledged her, and when Til chimed in, the two men were sucked into a one-sided conversation about her cosmetology internship. Apparently her name was "Stephaniegh", and she made sure to explain the spelling thoroughly to Jane. Jane couldn't bring herself to feign interest, and slipped out of the conversation once she was released from Stephaniegh's gripping discourse.

She lifted herself into a bar chair on the side of the table away from the crowd, and tried not to look ruffled when Cundo approached her. She caught Diego eyeing the two with interest from his side of the table.

"Diego said you wouldn't be here," she said finally, when it was clear that he wasn't removing his attention from her anytime soon.

"Ah," was all he said, pulling from his whiskey tumbler like it was beer. Jane didn't face him fully, but she couldn't help but look at him. Something happened to her insides when they locked eyes, and whether it was good or bad, Jane couldn't look away.

"I'm sorry for what I said," she blurted out, following it with a wince. What the hell?! Jane had never in her adult life apologized for anything unless it would gain her something. She did everything with deliberation and had no regrets, so there was nothing to feel sorry about. But something in her snapped, and she couldn't seem to piece it back together before she was saying unusual things to this man.

Cundo merely raised an eyebrow and tilted his head.

"What did you say?"

Oh God.

"You know...after our date. When I said that about your...face."

He kept looking at her.

"I really didn't mean it."

"I know." This took her by surprise.

"How do you know?"

"I figured you were lying," he said casually, crossing his arms over his barrelled chest. "In fact, I'm pretty sure you lie about a lot of things."

"I don't lie!" She lied defensively. Cundo smirked and leaned closer to her.

"I think you lie about everything."

I think you lie about everything.

Jane splashed some more water on her face and pulled in a shuddering breath. He was right. She did lie about everything. Every part of her life was constructed with untruths and dishonesty, built on a foundation of violence and revenge. Other than her plot for vengeance, she was empty; everything was a lie, a falsehood, a figment, and she was the miserable pin key in the middle of it all, holding her lies together.

As if a dam broke inside her, she choked out a sob and let hot tears rush out of her eyelids, cooling on her pale, trembling skin.

She was nothing. She was a killer, a taker of lives, and despite what she told herself, none of it had led to her ultimate goal yet. Her father's death went unpunished, and she was floating on aimless evil deeds of nothingness.

She let the sobs erupt out of her, succumbing to her self pity and pulling quick, loud breaths in and out. It was highly unattractive, she thought, watching herself fall apart in the mirror. She didn't even know how to cry appropriately, she looked disgusting.

In the mirror, she saw the bathroom door open behind her, and in walked Stephaniegh. She wrinkled her nose at Jane, and Jane ducked her head quickly, shielding her red, blotchy face from the view.

The woman didn't take long in the bathroom, and when she emerged to wash her hands in the rustic sink beside Jane, she watched her. Jane tried to keep her head down, but after the blonde dried her hands, she dipped her hand beneath Jane's curtain of hair and grasped her chin, pulling her face to her.

"He already dropped your ass, huh?" Stephaniegh said, studying her with inquisitive brown eyes.

"Who?"

"Diego. He does it pretty fast. Didn't think he'd do it in public in front of his friends, though," the woman's voice was fairly flat, but Jane thought she detected a note of sympathy.

"What? No," Jane pulled away, dabbing at her face with a wet paper towel. The blonde watched her for a second more before leaving.

Jane looked at herself in the dim lighting of the bathroom, studying each red spot, any out-of-place smudge of makeup, and the bright hazel eyes that stared back at her, the color heightened with the redness behind them. She supposed that she was beautiful- in general- but tonight, suffocating under the weight of the truth Cundo flung at her, she felt ugly. Repugnant. Hideous.

She pinched her cheeks to draw blood to the right places and smoothed her curls, regretting not bringing a ponytail to braid them back with. It was time to face the music. Taking another deep breath and praying that no one would notice the redness that remained in her eyes.

Cundo behaved casually as he made his way around his bar, ensuring that everything was running smoothly. Frank had no need of assistance at the bar as things died down, and the band had been handled and was packing up. He didn't know what to make of what Til's date, whatever her name was, had said when she came back from the bathroom. She'd stuck her finger in Diego's face and accused him of hurting Jane's feelings, more than likely projecting her own. Til had rolled his eyes and Diego had been all confusion, but Cundo swooped in to take the blame.

"It was me, I upset her," he'd said, earning shocked glances from the group. Til stuck his hand out for a fistbump and his date smacked him.

"Sorry," he said to Diego, shrugging.

"Well I hope you're sorry, because she was crying pretty hard in there," she said accusingly. Cundo set his drink down, trying not to look shocked. Jane? Crying? He somehow couldn't picture it. He turned to Diego.

"Hey, I know y'all need to get going, let me take her home," he grumbled. "I guess I need to make an apology."

Diego pursed his lips. "I don't want to get in the middle of this, whatever it is, but I'm pretty sure that she was trying to make you jealous tonight."

Cundo looked at him quizzically. Everyone was surprising him tonight.

Diego nodded. "She didn't show any interest in me- none whatsoever- until you showed up. She just wanted your attention."

"Well she has an interesting way of communicating that. The night we went out, she ended it by telling me-"

"I know," Diego cringed. "Til told me. I'm sorry, man...I'm not sure why she said that, but you guys need to talk it out."

They shook hands and said goodnight, the trio following the last of the customers out the door. Jane was emerging from the bathroom as they left, and Frank, a distance away behind the bar, disappeared into the kitchen, probably to leave before something exploded.

Jane looked around at the emptiness and approached Cundo at the bar table, looking lost.

"I guess I was in there for too long," she said, attempting a smile. Cundo noticed that her stormy eyes were cloudy, their usual brightness dulled with redness. Her little nose was red, her lips full. She was even beautiful when she cried. Ridiculous.

She didn't look like she was trying to appear as though she'd been crying, she looked like she was trying to hide it.

"Yeah, they took off. I told them I'd drive you home."

"I need my purse...I think I left it in Diego's car," she muttered nervously.

"Nope." He lifted it off the chair. "Right here."

They stood in silence for a beat.

"I told them I needed to talk to you so I could apologize."

She looked confused for a minute. "Are you going to?"

"No."

A look of relief crossed her face. He suppressed a smile.

"So what do you want with me?"

"I want to ask you what it is you're doing here." She looked nervous again.

"What do you mean?" she asked, her body forcibly relaxing and a sweet smile crossing her face. He scowled bitterly.

"Stop that."

"What?"

"Stop. That. Stop pretending with me. Or can you?" he asked sarcastically, watching as her body tensed back up, and she adopted a more authentic posture.

"Well what do you want me to be then?"

Cundo looked at her in shock and laughed without humor.

"Yourself. I mean, what the hell are you doing in this town? Do you even like it here? You creep around acting so sweet and innocent, but what are you even doing? No one really knows you. You said you'd get a job and you haven't. You talk about all these people you know and need to catch up with, but no one has spent more than an hour with you. What do you do, Jane?!"

He hadn't intended on making a delusional tirade, but he supposed it was best to get it out now while she already thought little of him. Jane looked taken aback, but more shocked than offended. Her gaze flickered over him as if seeing him for the first time, and he finally saw her through her opened-up stare, finally saw what she was hiding- pain.

She looked tired, weary, like a little kid that had been kept up far too long. The infantilization of herself stemmed from the child in her that had simply never left, and a part of him wanted to protect that child. Another part of him wanted to entice out the vicious, grown woman that he could sense existed in her. The one that lashed out with venom and quills- he wanted to know what else she had in her.

"Just talk to me," he said much more quietly, stepping towards her. Why was he begging this woman he didn't know nearly enough to get closer to him? He couldn't say.

She gazed up at him and almost looked like she was going to cry again. They were suddenly very close, and Cundo's breath was leaving him faster than he could pull it in.

"Talk?" she whispered. Their lips were too close.

Before he could take a moment to gather his thoughts and pull away, Jane's hands came up and with surprising strength pulled his face to hers. Their lips came crashing together with a bloodying force. Cundo winced at the pain, but couldn't stop his arms from encircling her and pulling her impossibly close.

Her caress was punishing, but almost reverent as she stroked her hands down his face, much bigger than her small hands. He grasped at her waist and groaned into her mouth when she pried his lips open with her tongue. She was fumbling and surprisingly inexperienced, but what she lacked in skill she made up for in raw, frenzied passion.

Before he knew it, he was pulling her towards the staircase that led up to his loft. She gave no resistance, and at her consent, he placed his hands beneath her thighs and hoisted her small body up against him to carry her up the stairs. He expected a girlish squeal when he trapped her against him, as most girls tended to do at a rough display of masculinity, but she let out a guttural moan and clasped her legs around his waist, pressing hard into his body.

He carried her up the stairs, expecting her to be light as a feather, but was pleasantly surprised when her seemingly soft body was hard and dense with muscle. Her thighs were like milk under his touch, soft and pliable, but when she locked herself around him, her muscles flexed into iron and stone. He growled in appreciation as he felt under her skirt.

Once they reached his bedroom, he prepared to drop her to the bed, but she leapt from his body and began removing his clothes for him. She started with his t-shirt, and he had to slow her hands so that her fervent grasp didn't tear the material. He chuckled, but stopped short when he saw the expression on her face. She appeared near tears.

He pulled her hands from her, clasping them to his chest and pulling her into a seated position on his bed.

"Sweetheart, what's wrong?" he asked in a hushed voice, brushing a hand over the crown of her head. She sighed and closed her eyes, leaning into his touch.

"Nothing's wrong."

"I don't believe that-"

"Nothing is wrong, everything is amazing. You feel amazing," she grabbed his face once more. "I have to do this before I get scared and stop."

Cundo pulled back. She leaned into him. "Are you scared of me?" It hurt to think that, but he wasn't sure what to think.

"No...I'm scared in general," she whispered against his chest. "I shouldn't tell you that, but I am. I'm fucking terrified."

He didn't know what to say, so he simply pulled her closer and wrapped his arms around her. They stayed like that for a while, and Cundo breathed in the smell of her hair. She smelled like hot sun, lemons, and jasmine.

"You don't have to be scared with me," he finally said, hesitant. "Whatever you're scared of, I would never let anything happen to you."

She pulled back just enough to look at him. Her eyes were dry, but she still looked open. He felt as if he could reach into her chest and feel her heartbeat at that very moment, and it would be real.

"I know," she said simply, and leaned in to take his lips against hers once more.

This time, they undressed each other gently, and took more time before working into the frenzied, desperate rush that had them pulling at each other with hot hands.

Jane pushed him back against the mattress, and he thanked himself for deciding to go with layers of sheets instead of a comforter for his bedspread—nothing was there to tangle against, it was just their bare bodies with an expanse of cotton supporting them.

He leaned back and let her take the lead, enjoying the view from below as she removed the last of her articles. She was magnificent, he realized, understanding now that she had never played on her beauty, but rather, dulled it.

Her orchid-petal skin came to raspberry-colored crests on her breasts, and her thighs parted over his own, creamy against his earth-colored skin, smattered with rough hair. She was so small compared to him, yet so completely in control. She clawed long, sharp fingernails down his chest, revelling at the expanse of him, and he hissed in pained satisfaction. Everything she did felt perfect.

She ran her palms, smooth aside from callouses on the index and middle fingers, along the sides of him, along the planes of his abdominal muscles and over his hips, where she brushed a hand across the hair that grew thicker as it reached his pelvic area. She backed down his legs and brushed herself along that part of him, relishing the feeling of him if her expression was any indication. Her slight body was malleable in some places and hard and taut in others. He stayed still for her as long as he could, but after more of her ministrations, he couldn't bear it any longer.

He grasped her upper arms and flipped her onto her back, rolling on top of her. She tensed at first, but when he leaned down to nestle his face against the crook of her neck, peppering kisses along her throat and shoulder, she relaxed, twisting her legs around him and locking her ankles together as if he was a tree branch catching her before a roaring waterfall. She held him tightly and rocked against him, letting out little gasping moans that sent a tingling sensation along the base of Cundo's spine.

"Jane," he moaned breathily against her neck, leaving open-mouthed kisses along her neck and working his way down her body, stopping at her breasts to administer light, teasing nuzzling that resulted in a primal, animalistic noise from her parted lips.

Cundo laughed against her body and rose from her to reach for his night stand. He paused and looked back at her. She looked disheveled and absolutely remarkable. Her pupils were dilated, her eyes heavy-lidded, and when her eyes caught sight of what he was reaching for, she nodded, a slow, certain smile spreading over her face. Thrills ran from the tips of his ears to the bottoms of his feet.

"This is...different for me," she said hesitantly as he rolled his condom on.

"What do you mean?"

"I've never done this...the way everyone else does it."

"We don't have to," he assured her quickly.

"No, I want to," she responded forcefully. "I want to do this the way other people do it, I want to know what it's like to be with someone you actually want."

At that, Cundo froze. What she said could mean a lot of things, but he could see the context in the determined set of her jaw and the tension in her body. She didn't know what it was like to be with someone willingly.

Cundo began to move away so he could explain to her that this wasn't necessary, and that they should take it slow, but she wasn't having any of it. She locked her lean legs around his thick body and pulled him back over her, pressing him to her core.

"You're different" she said softly, and he could hear the truth in her voice. "You feel safe."

Normally, a man wouldn't hear that and feel sexually invigorated, but Cundo felt her whispered confession down into his bones. He was her choice, after a lifetime without consensual interactions with men, he was what she wanted. Scars and all.

She pulled him down more gently, and he went eagerly, supporting his weight on his hands as he pressed into her. He needed to make this spectacular, worthy of her and worthy of the gift she was giving him.

He caressed her with hands and lips from the delicate skin of her face to the dusting of freckles on her shoulders to the feminine curves of her hips and downwards. After worshipping both full, muscled legs with his mouth, he dove into the most sacred place on her body and groaned loudly and shamelessly against her when he found her to be as in want of him as he was of her. She continued to make her animal sounds, grasping his hair and twisting his head around and around, uncaring as to how she moved him as long as she reached her goal. It was intoxicating to Cundo.

He brought her to the precipice and traveled back up the length of her body, aligning his with hers and searching her face. She seemed physically much smaller underneath him, but the presence in her eyes appeared larger than him, filling the room, as if he wouldn't be able to escape her even if he got out of bed and ran away right at that very moment.

He reached up to run a finger down her face, unblemished and untouched by the kind of violence that had ruined his own. She lifted her hand and did the same to him, then pulled him down to reach his lips. She hummed against his mouth as she tasted herself on his tongue. His kiss grew more desperate, eager to recreate that sound. He removed his hand from her face and reached down to grasp himself and align himself at her entrance.

Cundo looked into her eyes and waited for her cue. She set her jaw and braced her hands onto his shoulders. Then, out of nowhere, a devilish smile blossomed across her face and her eyes gleamed with the light of it. Something rushed through Cundo and he pushed into her, pausing when she flinched. Jane dug her nails into his shoulders and gritted her teeth against the discomfort, and Cundo -for the first time- cursed his own proportions. Soon, however, he was too overcome with sensation to consider that as Jane urged him deeper, and pinched her eyes closed. They wordlessly moved together, both sets of lungs clutching breath, not yet releasing.

"You are..." she hissed out on a breath. "So much better than I thought it would be."

Cundo groaned in response and began to move. Their bodies danced together in a writhing, earthly dance. The humidity in the room rose and their figures were enveloped in a cloud of steam that seemed to rise from their bodies, becoming smoke emanating from the friction between them, the hard and rough planes of Cundo's body caressing and stilling the softer hills and valleys of Jane's, pumping into her as if he could rid her of her past with the force of his need for her.

"God..." he grumbled, his voice muffled by her neck, which was damp with both of their perspiration. Jane huffed in agreement, growing frantic and frustrated, using her hands to pull him into her, fingers digging into the muscle of his backside. The keening moans and animalistic sounds coming from her spurred him on- he hadn't held a woman who showed this kind of desire for him in so long, and a woman like Jane- a beautiful woman with mystery and power so physical that anyone that saw her wanted her- and Cundo had her.

They raced one another to a crescendo, and he worked hard on her body to repay the cost of what she was giving him in spades. The ecstasy on her face was enough in itself to push him over the edge.

They reached the apex of their ardor one after the other; first Jane in a frenzied hurricane of gratification, then Cundo in a beautiful disaster shortly after. As disorganized and frantic as their coupling had been, it seemed to Cundo that they'd created a masterpiece together- the midst of it a Jackson Pollock of chaos, and the peace and satisfaction that came after- a Rothko. One of his colder pieces, blues and greys. Greys and steels. Steel grey sheets kicked to the floor- panting, sizzling bodies coming down from their high together.

The beauty of their odd, unspoken connection was that they could lay in unattractive, unromantic, but very pleased afterglow without any pretense of composure. Jane sprawled out, eyes closed and mouth open, breathing heavily but never losing her grin. Cundo panted equally hard, not caring to collect himself to pose with bored masculinity. He was thrilled, and he felt that he could reveal that to Jane.

Jane suddenly inched closer to him and threw one leg over his, her knee overlapping his much larger thigh, coarse with hair. She laid her arm across his chest, still on her back, and Cundo lay very still, not wanting to disturb her. A small grin stole over his lips as he closed his eyes and simply enjoyed her silent presence beside him. Though it had been a while, he was familiar with this- the exhaustion combined with the need to touch, the simple, basic need to have contact with your partner. She didn't move, but kept her leg over his, and slowly ran her fingers over his abdomen. Cundo watched the outline of her form in the darkness, listening to her breath grow even with sleep.

CHAPTER 12

Orca, Orcinus orca

Jane blinked her eyes open to the early morning light filtering in through the loft windows. She squinted against the sun and turned her head to the side- that's when she saw him.

She knew logically that she'd slept with Cundo last night, but with the gorgeous evidence right there beside her- the sandstone color of his skin practically glowing in the sunlight- she shivered. Dust particles drifted lazily around them, visible only because of the lack of curtains over his windows. She wanted to stroke a hand down the scars on his face, but she didn't want to wake him and disturb this perfect moment of peace.

The sensation she felt, staring at Cundo's relaxed features, reveling in the delicious soreness of her body, rivalled anything she'd experienced before. Painting gave her a sense of wholeness, killing gave her the thrill of power- but lying there beside the beast of a man that had destroyed and rebuilt her world the night before was another animal entirely.

It was almost like need, but it was simpler than that, more base. She knew that she didn't truly need him and that felt good, to be with someone for no reason other than a simple desire to be. It was alien to her and almost frightening. She allowed herself to relish the feeling, knowing that the fear and logic of emotional obstacles would come for her later. Right now, she would simply examine this new development.

Perhaps the feeling of her eyes boring into him finally stirred him, or perhaps it was the uncomfortable heat of two bodies intertwined under direct sunlight, but Cundo opened his eyes and rolled over. His massive body caused the sturdy bed frame to creak as he slung an arm over her and nuzzled his face against the top of her head.

"What time is it?" he mumbled into her hair, and Jane closed her eyes for a brief second, wondering if this was what it would be like to be a normal woman in the arms of a lover.

"Nine," she replied, glancing at the analog clock on his bedside table. She hadn't taken him for a lover of vintage things, but the aesthetic of his loft included a small selection of antiques, no twenty-first century technology, and a minimalist, industrial look that she would not have attributed to him. Perhaps it was the kinds of men she'd met in her life, but she'd expected him to have a dart board on the wall, box springs directly on the floor, and perhaps a couple posters of suggestively-posed women. This space, however, looked like it was meant to be a retreat from business and life.

"I like your place," she said softly, tentatively stroking the back of his head as he began to drop kisses along her shoulder.

"Thanks," his voice was muffled, for he seemed reluctant to stop kissing her. She knew she would have to face the impracticality of their arrangement sooner or later, but for now, she couldn't help but appreciate the strange thrill it gave her to luxuriate in bed with this man. She felt deliciously exposed without a trace of a costume, her clothes on the floor and her makeup rubbed off, curls spread wildly about her. She was her most naked self, and to have Cundo merely be his naked self with her was a privilege she'd never partaken in before.

"Do you have to get up?" she asked, not wanting to wake them from this dream-like space but knowing that he had a job to do.

"No," he said simply, and continued brushing his lips along her figure, moving down to trace her collarbone.

"Good," she replied honestly, and he let out a surprised laugh. His laugh made him seem much younger.

At that thought, she asked, "How old are you?" Cundo stopped kissing and looked up at her. She wrinkled her nose and he smirked, placing a conciliatory peck on her cheek.

"Thirty-two. You?"

"Sixteen."

He laughed and reached up to tug on one of her curls. "Seriously, Jane."

"I'm twenty-four."

He let out a low whistle and rolled over.

"So I guess I'm a cradle-robber then," he said jokingly. She twisted her lips.

"You're nothing of the sort," she said with distaste. He furrowed his brow and sat up.

"Just a joke, Jane."

Cundo stood and pulled some things out of his dresser drawer, slipping on a pair of boxer briefs that hugged his muscular thighs and gave Jane more ideas about what to do with him.

"Do you want some breakfast?"

Jane pulled her gaze away from his body to nod, and Cundo disappeared out of the room to fulfill the promise. Once he was gone, Jane could take a better look around the space, noticing that not many personal items were in view. A small leather chest lay on his dresser with a candle, a decorative vase, and a nondescript ring of keys. Jane knew she shouldn't pry, but with it being the only thing of consequence in the room, she had to open it. After all, investigating mysterious men was one of her many interests.

The box was trouble to open, but once it popped open with a squeak, she carefully shifted the items around inside. Some photos, ticket stubs, medals, pins, and a bracelet lie inside. She lifted the bracelet and fingered the white beads, noticing the worn glaze on a couple of them. She picked a photograph next, staring at a beautiful woman with long, straight hair and a baby on her hip. Her smile was stunning, matching that of the laughing baby she held. The baby's curly hair was the antithesis of her own, but it was clear that they were mother and son. On the back of the photo, scrawled in slanted, cursive handwriting were the words "Maria and Cundo."

A tingle ran down her spine, and Jane dropped the photo, clutching the sheet she'd dragged with her closer to her chest. It was obviously a coincidence, but the first thing that ran through her mind was Phillip Caruther's "suicide note"...Maria...you and your son...you were good to me...

"You found my mother."

Jane jumped away from the box, uncharacteristic guilt overcoming her at snooping through his personal items. She closed the box quickly and stepped away.

Cundo placed two coffee mugs on his bedside table and came over to reopen the box and remove the picture she'd been looking at. His expression was unreadable.

"She's beautiful," Jane said lightly, not sure how to react to getting caught.

Cundo nodded and touched the photo gently, "She was." Ah.

"What happened?" She almost didn't want to know, but perhaps if she heard that her suspicions weren't true from his lips, she would be able to bury the grisly truth about herself and enjoy this with Cundo for a little while longer.

Cundo stared at the picture for a moment before looking her in the eye. Making eye contact was almost too much for her, her skin growing hot. She clutched the sheet around her.

"You really want to know?" She nodded. "She was killed."

Interest and surprise registered on his face, and she wondered why before realizing that she hadn't reacted to his statement.

"Oh, my...I'm so sorry," she said, her late reaction causing Cundo to narrow his eyes and close the box. For some reason, she felt eager to repair the connection they'd been enjoying moments ago. "I'm sorry, I wish I could be shocked, it just feels normal to me."

Why was she explaining herself?

"Murder?" Cundo quipped dryly with a bitter grin, handing one of the mugs to her. She inhaled over the rim and was surprised to smell her favorite morning tea- plantation mint- instead of coffee.

"Well, you know my dad was killed. And being in the foster system, I saw a lot of weird stuff. It's just not surprising anymore. I am sorry, though. How old were you?"

Cundo took a long sip of his coffee before answering. "Seventeen." The skin along her spine tingled again.

"Who did it?"

She didn't mean to ask that, but she did want to know. Cundo sat down on his bed and studied her.

"A lot of people thought I did it for a while." He kept watching her and Jane got the feeling that he wanted to unsettle her with that statement. He didn't.

"Why would they think that?"

"Because I had a temper as a kid. I was big. I was also there...and then I ran." They kept watching each other, daring the other to be uncomfortable with the interrogation, like a psychotic game of chicken.

"So who really did it?"

Cundo looked out the window, losing the game.

"You know that guy in town...the one that killed himself?"

Her spine lit on fire with the lightning bolt she'd sensed earlier. Too much. Too close.

"The coach?" she replied nonchalantly.

"Yeah. He wasn't a coach then. He had a different name." Jane watched as Cundo's eyes grew distant. "I don't know why I'm telling you this."

"It's okay, keep going." She needed to hear it. She was screaming on the inside.

"He did it. They were looking for him. It's been so long...I figured he'd died somewhere, gotten caught up on another charge...I don't know. I guess I just never thought he could be living a completely different life somewhere. He never should've been allowed to live past the moment he killed my mother."

The coldness in Cundo's gaze and tone sent a thrill through her.

"It's okay, he's gone now," she reassured him, her reassurance being complete in a way that Cundo couldn't possibly understand. She yearned to tell him that it was her, she was the one that had brought him to justice.

"I was there the night he died," Cundo said distantly, and Jane froze. Had he seen her? Was he going to reveal that he knew her secret and demand compensation for his silence? Her mind ran with possibilities until Cundo spoke again.

"I almost killed him." They sat silent for a second, and Jane got the feeling that Cundo was doing two things- both unburdening himself to her, and testing her to see if she could handle the intensity of his thoughts. His life. If only he knew.

Instead of answering, she set down her tea and crawled into his lap. Cundo wrapped himself around her gratefully, and she once again wondered at the tenderness exchanged between them.

"Do you ever feel like you're a completely different person than you think you are?" he asked.

Jane nodded against his chest. "I know that if I died tomorrow, no one, including myself, would have ever really met me."

"Hey," he said, jostling her a bit. "I can tell that things...have happened to you. I just want you to know that you're safe with me."

"I know."

Cundo pulled her to a standing position and drew her to the entrance of his bedroom.

"Come on, I made tacos."

Cundo drove Jane home in his big, chrome-detailed pick-up, and Jane kept the window rolled down, the desert air of late morning gliding over her in her sundress from the night before, bare feet kicked up on the dashboard. Their hands were folded together on the console, and Cundo was drawing circles on the back of her hand with his thumb, and every movement sent chills through her.

When he pulled up to her father's cabin, Cundo let out a small grunt of frustration.

"I guess I'll let you go," he said bitterly, thrusting his gear shift into park.

Jane laughed at his pout. "We'll see each other soon."

"Will we?"

Their gazes connected and she nodded, smiling.

It wasn't until he'd backed down her driveway and disappeared in a dust cloud on the dirt road that she made her way to the back of the house where she found a man sitting in her mother's old rocking chair on the porch.

"Officer Lasica?" she asked in confusion, masking her defensiveness with a sugary sweet surprise.

"Hey there, Janie," the older man said with a smile that crinkled his eyes. He rose to give her a hug that disturbed her like it had at the diner. "I wanted to come by and drop something off...I thought about taking it directly to the precinct, but I wanted to give you some closure...you can do with it what you want."

Jane was about to invite him inside out of an automatic display of false civility, but she realized that she didn't want to. Her night with Cundo had her feeling eager to be her authentic self, and Officer Lasica didn't fit into her portrait.

"Thank you," she said, simply retrieving the manila envelope that he held out, and said her goodbyes without a pretense of politeness.

She waited until she heard his car start and distance itself before opening the envelope.

CHAPTER 13

South American Green Anaconda, Eunectes murinus

Jane drummed her fingers on her steering wheel, shaking her leg. She'd spent the entire day before going over the file that Lasica had dropped off. With trembling hands, she'd opened it. How, she wondered, could she have gone all this time without this information when she felt so suffocated and desperate with the information actually in her hand?

Her first instinct, after only one night, was to call Cundo. To do so would be to reveal the intricacies of her hunt, the details that went into her scene, and it would slowly unravel her history of killing.

Cundo may be an ex-marine, hardened and a casualty of his mother's murder, but there was a nearly nonexistent chance of him understanding the way she'd lived her life. She needed to go about this on her own.

Which is how she wound up parked in front of Aunt Cookie's Cafe, a diner stationed in a lone, mobile building along a highway. The majority of the occupants seemed to be truckers, if the eighteen-wheelers parked in the field beside it were any indication. Her truck was among a handful of other beat-up pick-ups in the cramped parking lot. She wasn't sure why she'd decided to come here first, maybe because if she faced the man himself, she knew she wouldn't be able to do it.

The file had contained a couple names, a little information, a brief, written confession, and nothing more.

Jacob Diaz, age 42, hospice care at St. Ann's Texas Hospice Center.

One living relative, Esmerelda Diaz, age 19.

She couldn't re-read the confession without developing tremors all over, so instead, she focused on the windows of the diner, wondering if she'd have to go inside to catch a glimpse of her.

A hospice nurse that had become close to Jacob Diaz had obtained the confession- the cartel had fingers in the towns running through West Texas, and Detective Fairweather had his own finger on their pulse. Jacob Diaz wasn't a part of the cartel or even any affiliated people, but he did owe money to some of them, and that put him in a dangerous position- a useful one to his creditors. Lasica had included information on her father's connection to the cartel, but it simply didn't fit. If her father was affiliated with them and had simply displeased them, they would have sent a footman to do so much more than shoot one bullet in order to make a point. In the seedy underbelly of small towns with criminal histories, Jane had learned how far those in organized crime would go to teach someone a lesson.

Jacob Diaz was supposed to make it look like a simple B and E, and leave no witnesses. He gave what he'd stolen to his creditors and left town with his daughter, his life, and a lack of debt. He'd returned to raise her closer to their family as he'd fallen ill, and it seemed that he was hoping to unburden his daughter if the state took him into custody. His nurse decided that he would take the information directly to the officer who'd been on the case prior to retirement as requested and let everything pan out.

Why Lasica had delivered the information to her instead of to the precinct, she couldn't be sure. Had he thought she wouldn't be able to stomach turning in a dying man? Did he think this would convince her of her father's corruption? And if so, why would he leave the choice up to her if it wouldn't lead to justice?

These questions ran through Jane's head as she stared into the diner. She pulled her phone out once more and opened it to the social media page she'd been examining. Esmerelda Diaz, age 19.

Esmerelda, or "Mel" was beautiful, all long curls and big, chocolate eyes. There were no pictures of her with friends, as Jane had figured when she discovered the girl was responsible for her father's medical bills. There were a couple pictures of her with her father, who lay, pale and sickly in a hospital bed. Mel was a contrast to the ghost in the bed, a picture of health and life. She'd shared articles and pages about some kind of blood disorder, and Jane felt a sort of kinship with the girl. She herself would have been at her father's side, learning and doing everything she could to help him, had he ever been this ill. Jane looked at her birthday on her "about" information several dozen times, the information that revealed where she works. She would've been about nine when her father killed Jane's.

Jane forced herself to put her phone away and tucked the papers from the file, folded neatly, into her pocket. She exited the vehicle with numb hands.

She'd been searching for her father's killer for so long that she wasn't sure what to do with this information. She'd thought of a million different scenarios; a man in a dangerous gang, a dead body with a little extra cash and a gun, a small-time mugger who would get busted for another B and E...the ideas she'd had had never included an apologetic, dying man. Much less one with a daughter.

Jane entered the diner, setting off a little chime above the door. The diner wasn't too brightly lit, so her eyes had to adjust from the brilliant Texas sun outside. As predicted, the ballcap-covered heads of truckers filled the booths, a couple elderly couples smattered here and there. Across the diner, at the counter, a woman spoke with a cashier. Jane didn't believe in auras, but she immediately recognized the woman because of hers. Her long hair had been pulled back in a braid, and her boxy waitress uniform couldn't hide her elegant movements. Jane watched for a minute before taking a seat at the counter and opening a nearby menu.

"Howdy, welcome to Aunt Cookie's. Is there anything I can get you?" Jane heard over her shoulder. She looked back to find Mel smiling brightly at her, notepad in hand.

"A sweet tea would be great," she responded tremulously. Mel nodded and brightly noted that she'd get it right away, hopping towards the kitchen. Jane could see her body sag and her smile drop just before she disappeared around the corner.

That woman is the reason Jane was alive.

That was the conclusion she'd come to after spending a painful night before reliving her father's murder. She'd forced herself to consider every detail, every last minute of the noises she'd heard, the sights she'd seen, the man standing in the center of her living room with a gun pointed at her father and a sorrowful expression on his face.

That face.

He'd looked horrified to see her. He'd dropped his gun and he had to pick it back up before rushing out of the house like the hounds of hell were on his heels. There was no doubt in Jane's mind that he'd had trouble bringing himself to kill a man, but had a complete barrier on the path to killing a child. Stumbling on a young girl in the middle of a kill, a mere five years older than his own daughter, had more than likely scarred him. Certainly no more scarring than seeing your father murdered, of course.

Mel appeared with her sweet tea and asked if she could get Jane anything else. Jane studied her for a moment. Her smile was beatific, and Jane wondered how such beauty could have sustained itself in the withering, hot dust of the cartels in West Texas. Jane's inner beauty had fallen face-first into darkness the moment her father was killed, and yet this young woman remained...stunning.

"I'd like the chorizo and egg plate," she said, instead of, "How are you like this?"

Mel seemed grateful for the simple order and left to fill it. Her father was dying, and who knows what means she was resorting to in order to pay his hospice bills. Perhaps Jane should give the information to the police and relieve her of the burden he carried.

But something in Jane didn't want this girl to find out that the man she'd do anything to keep alive just a little longer was a killer. She knew that she couldn't bear for any future children of her own to consider her evil to that degree, no matter how justified it felt to her.

Jane ate her breakfast because it seemed to keep the smile on Mel's face and left a healthy tip before leaving.

On the drive back to the outskirts of her own town, Jane rolled down the window and let the hot air billow around her, muffling the sound of The Four Seasons coming from her speakers. She wished there was an easier answer to the silent question of what she would do. She'd waited years to discover this information, years to return to her town, years of exercise in killing villains of the night, years of learning how to infiltrate the day to her advantage, months of planning the re-acquirement of her childhood home and what she would do if she managed to find what she'd needed.

She'd waited so long, and now she didn't know what to do.

She'd always assumed that if she'd discovered that her father's killer was innocent aside from that one particular night, she would still have no qualms about ending his life.

But after years of digging up the lowest, most vile dregs of humanity, she'd realized that there were degrees of evil, and her black-and-white perception had to develop exceptions. She could torment a mugger who steals from the vulnerable and turn him in to the police, but she wouldn't kill him- not when there were rapists to disembowel.

Where did Jacob Diaz fall on the scale?

. . .

"Good afternoon," Cundo said cheerfully to a couple that had just walked into the bar. He'd given Frank the day off and was reliving his bartending career behind the glossy mesquite bar, wiping down glasses and experimenting with new flavors. He hadn't been in such a gloriously good mood in years.

Til scowled at him from his stool, pulling from his beer instead of chattering away like he usually did. Cundo didn't care what Til thought of his friend's opinion on his new relationship with Jane- his only concern was what Jane thought. She hadn't returned his call, and he wasn't confident enough in what they'd shared to call again, but that couldn't dampen the upbeat attitude that had overcome him from the moment he took Jane in his arms.

Diego had shown up to check on Cundo in person, wondering how things had gone. The ever-present grin spread over Cundo's ruined face gave him an idea.

"I was wondering if you wanted to hang out at the range this weekend," Diego mentioned from his seat beside the sulking Til. Shooting had been one of their bonding activities both during and after active duty. It brought Cundo a sense of peace to lose himself in a firearm with his brothers by his side, and peace wasn't something he found often on his own.

"Can I bring Jane?" Cundo asked immediately, kicking himself mentally. *Why would you ask that, she hasn't even returned your call? And what if she doesn't shoot recreationally?*

Diego chuckled, "It wouldn't be weird for you?" Cundo had forgotten that Jane and Diego were the ones that were supposed to be on a date that night.

"Oh, nah, I don't care if you don't."

Diego smirked and nodded, glancing at Til who rolled his eyes.

"You in, buddy?"

"Sure, whatever," Til grumbled into his bottle.

CHAPTER 14

Texas Mountain Lion, Puma concolor

Cundo chastised himself for being so nervous. He'd been practically shaking when he worked up the nerve to call Jane a second time, and practically threw up when she answered. She'd sounded distracted, but he couldn't deny the pleasure he heard in her tone as she agreed to come to the shooting range with them. He'd been surprised when he asked if she needed hearing protection and she said she'd bring her own. "Nothing like a woman that brings her own protection," Diego had said.

That Saturday, as he turned off the asphalt of the access road and onto the dirt road that would eventually lead to Jane, he glanced at the time and cursed himself. He'd been so eager that he'd overestimated the time and he'd be arriving a half hour early like some kind of psychopath, but he couldn't pull up to her house and simply wait. That would make him look like more of a psychopath.

Her cabin looked a little fresher than it had when he'd picked her up for their first date. He imagined that the potted plants hanging from the front porch and the new paint job on the swing were her way of bringing the place back to life. He smiled at that.

She didn't answer the front door, and he'd remembered seeing her disappear around the back to go inside when he'd dropped her off the morning before, so he tentatively made his way to the back door, hoping not to scare her. Before he could raise his hand to knock, he heard a rustling behind him and turned to see Jane emerging from a shed in the back property. She grabbed a color-splattered drop cloth off the ground and began pulling it inside.

She dropped the material when she raised her head and caught sight of him. She looked shocked, but quickly plastered on a smile for him.

"Hey, you," she chirped, hopping over the drop cloth to come to him. She grew more shy the closer she got, and stopped in front of him. Cundo realized that he'd been simply staring at her, taking in the tumbling mass of golden curls she'd piled on her head and the paint-splattered overalls that she wore with nothing but a thin bra underneath.

"Hey..." he replied belatedly, trailing off. She stepped a bit closer, and the connection they'd shared so recently sparked back to life in the charged air between them. He reached for her face and brushed aside one of the rogue curls.

Without another word, they dove for one another's mouths and grabbed at each other with frenzied need. Cundo hooked a finger in each side of her overalls and pulled her closer to him, needing to remember that she was real and tangible. The bare skin under her overalls was soft, hot, and damp with imminent perspiration, and Cundo had the sudden and overwhelming urge to be the one to make her sweat.

Before he could pull the fastenings from her overalls like a caveman, she pulled away with a grin.

"I have to go get ready, I didn't think you would be here so soon," she said, her voice giving him goosebumps.

"Okay," he said dumbly, watching her disappear into the house. He tried to calm himself by remaining on the porch and looking out over the property her cabin resided on. Her taxes must be incredible, he thought, watching light glance off the low, still tank that spread out over some of the land. She must've gone swimming in the tank as a child. He wondered briefly what it would be like to raise a child on this property.

Then he caught sight of the shed.

He hadn't known she was a painter, but being an artist might explain some of her more unusual character traits. Perhaps she thought she had to put on a show for people in order to pass as one of the simple, conservative country girls that had grown up in Fort Zemsta. He wanted to see her paintings.

Without a second thought, propelled only by the need to know more about the woman he intended to lay with again, he crossed to the shed and entered it, picking up her drop cloth and folding it for her. It had smooth flakes of dry paint coming from it, and other, stickier materials that came off on his hands. Inside the shed, there was a table set up with a desktop computer, and boxes of every kind- transparent and plastic, full of art supplies, cardboard boxes, black lock boxes, file boxes...all lining the walls and supporting stacks of covered canvases that seemed to be of every shape and size. He moved over to a stack of small ones, not much larger than his hands, but paused when he passed her makeshift desk.

Atop it lay a wireless router and a number of thick cords that seemed to provide something to the desktop, but surrounding the keyboard were pieces of paper and manila filing folders. An extremely well-used notepad was open to a blank page.

His hands itched to look at the notepad, but he knew it was wrong. Even if there weren't secrets he shouldn't know between its pages, it was still wrong to look without asking.

He wondered at the fact that she hid her office in a shed. Was there no Ethernet connection in her house? Or was there a more private reason?

Cundo shook that thought out of his head and turned to leave.

But then he couldn't.

This is the first woman he'd trusted in years- the first woman that hadn't flinched from his scars in horror. The first woman he wanted something with past one night.

He needed to know if she was hiding something.

He turned and deftly flipped through the pages, trying to read quickly so he could leave the shed without alerting her to his prying.

The things he read on the pages didn't make sense. One page had different names of stores and places of business in town, and one had a very detailed account of what appeared to be a children's baseball game. Then he flipped to the next page.

Phillip Caruthers.

The name had been written several times, his alias's name written below it.

Dates, locations, a license plate number, and a Saturday through Sunday schedule of his whereabouts appeared in the following pages. Cundo flipped through them with a growing sense of dread. His first thought was that Jane had learned everything she could about Caruthers after Cundo had told her that he'd killed Cundo's mother, but the details went so much further- how would she have found his license plate? There were a full two weeks of detailed observations on his behavior and schedule- written in present tense.

Cundo grew feverish, flipping through the pages. Why? Why, why, why, why... He couldn't believe what he was seeing. There were more names, the names of men he'd never heard of. More details, more information, information on her father and his murder. Cundo was near tears when he heard the back door of the cabin slam shut.

He flipped the notebook back to the blank page and moved to fiddle with the drop cloth he'd folded.

"Hey!" He turned to find Jane, sweet Jane, smiling at him with a note of tension in her face. "Thanks for picking that up."

"Of course," he said, looking away from her.

As they left the shed, Jane used two different keys and a combination to close up the shed. Her jaw was locked, and despite her smile, Cundo could tell that she was displeased he'd been in her space.

Cundo escorted her to his truck and pushed everything he'd just seen to the back of his mind in order to focus on her in the moment- he'd become an expert on that during his service. All of his concerns about strategy, an injured man, his own injuries, their food supply, all of it would disappear when he became focused enough. He had to be focused.

"You look different today," he observed, and Jane stiffened as she hauled a black bag and a gun case into his backseat. Her outfit consisted of boots, jeans, and a loose t-shirt that cascaded over her curves in a far more romantic way than he thought possible for a simple cotton t-shirt.

"What do you mean?"

"In a good way," he added hurriedly. "I've just never seen you in jeans before."

"Yeah, well I wear them."

They got in the car, and Cundo let out a small sigh. Their earlier chemistry had been swallowed up by the secrets Jane was hiding in her shed, and she clearly wasn't relenting. He wished she would give him an explanation that cleared things up so they could go back to reveling in each other, but she was silent.

Cundo was usually much more comfortable with silence, but hers was unnerving at this moment. He wanted to ask her so many questions, but he didn't know if he could handle the answers. What if she'd known Phillip

Caruthers? What if they were involved somehow? There was no way she wasn't involved in something sinister with what he'd seen in her notes.

He attempted to make small talk with her, and he managed to sound relaxed enough that she too loosened up. He asked her what sort of gun she'd brought with her, and was surprised to hear how many she'd packed into the briefcase-sized gun case. She'd brought all of her own supplies, including her own ammo.

"Well, there's no need for that, Diego keeps a ton at the range."

"He stores it there?"

"Well, yeah," then realization dawned on him. "Ah. See, it's his range."

Jane whipped her head around to him.

"It's his?" she asked, shocked. Cundo realized that this was the first time he'd seen her surprised in any way.

"Yeah, is that okay? I know he's fine with how things played out between you, and I definitely am, but-"

"No, don't worry about it," she said casually. "I just didn't know he owned a range. That's so cool."

"Well don't think it's too cool, I don't want to have to win you back from him again," he said laughingly, only half joking. She smiled slyly.

"Don't worry about that. I am not won, I am earned."

. . .

Jane was further surprised when they arrived at the range and were greeted with a cool, industrial interior that sported buffalo plaid and wood accents. She'd assumed that a male-owned business would be ramshackle and unappealing, but it was designed to make the consumer feel at home. Cundo carried her gun case along with his own, despite her protests, and set them down on the wide, mesquite counter to do the bro-hug with his friends. Til and Diego were present, but Frank, as Cundo had said, was home with his wife and baby.

Diego greeted her congenially, but Til simply nodded to her and kept his distance. She would worry about that some other time.

"Alright, Janie, are you ready to get your butt kicked by some Marines?" Diego bellowed, grabbing an ammo bucket from behind the corner and taking off.

Jane startled at the nickname, and looked at Cundo. He rolled his eyes and grabbed their stuff.

"It's not a competition," he reassured her, but when he turned around, a slow smile crept over her face.

This would be fun.

The stalls were indoor, so even with ear protection, the tinny pops of gunfire echoed through the space. It was wide open, with lots of space between and behind the shooters, leaving plenty of room for the men to set up, to her surprise, chips and salsa on one of the tables behind them.

"I made my dip," Til said, still concealing all emotion behind a pout, and laid a tupperware of seven layer dip on the table.

"Yeeessss," hissed Diego in satisfaction. "Alright, Jane, so Cundo tells us that you brought your own guns. How often do you shoot?"

Jane pretended to consider it, even though she had a strict regimen of physical exercise and self-defense practice, which included shooting.

"Hm, I don't know. Three to four times a week, maybe?"

Cundo looked at her sharply, not expecting her answer. Jane smirked at him before plopping her gun case on the table and entering the combination to open it.

Diego whistled. "That's a lot of time, chica. You must be pretty good. Think you're as good as a Sergeant Major from the Marine Corps?"

"You were a sergeant major?"

"No," Diego laughed. "Your boy toy over there was."

Cundo scowled at Diego as Jane looked at him with a new admiration. She'd known his years in the service had been difficult, and that he'd medically retired early, but she hadn't known he'd been a sergeant major. He had to have been promoted at a fairly young age.

"Where did you serve primarily?"

"Iraq," Cundo replied brusquely. He hadn't exactly been forthcoming about his time as a Marine, but Jane had assumed it was because he was like all the other early "vets" that hadn't resigned their commission and his time hadn't been too impactful. Iraq had shaken people all the way back to America, down into their little town of Fort Zemsta, where airforce vets lived to tell their tales to newly deployed airmen. But Cundo was an anomaly- a young man with an old man's stories.

She didn't say anything, but donned her ear and eye protection and watched him as he assembled an M4 with ease, barely looking at the pieces.

"So we're shooting rifles today?"

"Yup," Diego said, punching numbers into a panel on the stall's wall and sending the papers he'd clipped onto the overhanging cord to the farthest reaches of the warehouse. He pulled a couple of rods out from underneath the stand in the stall, and allowed it to drop down to table height, pulling up a chair and plopping sand bags onto its top.

"But you're free to shoot handguns next to us. I'll keep the papers at, what do you want, six yards?"

Jane snorted. "Sure, if I'm shooting with a slingshot."

Cundo and even Til erupted in a chorus of oooohhs, before Diego shushed them and sent her papers out twenty-five yards.

"There you go, princess, let's see how you do."

Jane rolled her eyes and pulled out her princess, her Glock .40, and slipped a full clip into her gun. The satisfying sound that came with cocking the gun and loading the chamber lit a familiar fire in her. She looked back to see the three men watching her, waiting to see how she did.

She made sure to turn back to the target before she grinned.

Her feet shoulder-width apart, arms up and relaxed, front sight aligned with the point just below the center of her target, she inhaled, and...

Out came a breath.

Out came a bullet.

The kick of her gun is like the jumpstart in a race. Things moved slowly for her, everything rolling easily- a drizzle of smoke curling from the barrel, the brass casing escaping the ejection port and tinkling to the ground, the papers, 25 yards away, rippling at the impact, and her hands, repositioning the gun to fire again.

Rapid fire.

Typically frowned upon at a range, but with the owner giving her leave to do as she wished and two marines looking on, she fired at will, shifting infestimally to accomplish the design she was creating on the paper. Her grin grew, and her eyes, razor-focused and unblinking, remained narrowed-in on the paper.

Her mind went back to a particularly thrilling kill one year in college- she'd chased a campus predator down with his own gun, one that had been held to the temple of one too many young, unwilling girls. That one-too-many being Jane.

She'd shot in complete darkness, fog, pouring rain, and blinding daylight. The functional lighting of the indoor range was child's play, and her 20/20 vision captured every last detail as she shot.

When she liberated her magazine of its sixteenth round, she wasted no time in pressing the magazine release with her right hand as she reached for a fresh clip at her hip with her left, bringing it up to fill the hollow grip just as it relinquished the empty one.

She pulled the slide back and returned to firing once more, the pause giving her just enough time to catch the murmuring of the men around her as her shots echoed metallically.

Once she'd finished emptying the second clip, she released it and slammed her hand on the retrieval button for the papers.

She turned and hopped back to the table with a pep in her step.

"I feel so spoiled," she giggled. "Usually I have to go pick up my own papers."

The men ignored her and gaped at the papers that were swinging to a stop in front of the stall. Two bullet holes imitated eyes on the head of the silhouette on the paper, a line of them curling into a gruesome smile beneath them. A cluster of holes that created one larger one rested in its forehead, and a much larger cluster resided over its heart. The overall effect was rather ghastly, and Jane wondered if this would give Cundo another reason to be suspicious of her on top of her unusual shed. She decided that the look on the men's faces was worth the risk.

"God damn," Til exclaimed, taking the papers down and feeling the holes. "How long have you been shooting?"

"Since I was strong enough to pick up a handgun," she quipped, and Cundo swung his gaze to her. Instead of suspicion, hot desire burned in his eyes. He quirked his eyebrow up, the scarred one, pulling the edges taut. She grinned back.

"I thought you were a counselor," Diego said suspiciously, revealing less of his thoughts than Til.

"I'm allowed to have hobbies," Jane replied in faux defense.

"Well, we'll have to come by and indulge in our hobbies together more often," Cundo interjected in a low voice that made Jane question which hobbies he was referring to.

The men settled their compliments towards Jane's shooting, and began to subtly flex their masculinity with their own weapons. Diego took the M4 that Cundo had been assembling and set up shop in front of his stall. Jane had assumed that they would shoot the papers that had been wheeled to the other end of the warehouse, but there was an open bar of light shining into the outdoor range- metal shutters had been opened, and Jane could see the targets posted to hay bales at 600 yards.

Jane watched Diego for a minute before observing Til in the next stall. He was wielding an Avtomat Kalashnikova with deadly accuracy, revealing a focus that Jane didn't expect of him. With unblinking eyes focused on the scope, this was the most still she'd ever seen him. She wondered what his background with firearms was.

Then she got to Cundo. He'd assembled another M4, but he was taking his time lowering the counter in front of him in his stall. He glanced at her lazily, picking up a small magazine and loading it.

"What are you shooting first?" Jane asked, leaning around him and putting her hand on the small of his back. She didn't normally initiate contact, it being something she typically dreaded, but she would use any excuse she could to get closer to him and explore the emotions she experienced in his presence.

He moved away from her and she felt a stab of disappointment, but then he reached around to the small of his back and removed a Beretta from the hidden holster tucked into his jeans. His shirt lifted with the motion, a motion that sent a bolt of lightning down through her belly, and Jane saw an expanse of scar tissue stretched over hard muscle. The scars in that area were shiny and pale, less sun damage than the ones on his face, but gruesome nonetheless. The only thing Jane could think of was how much further she could drag up his shirt without him noticing.

He gently urged her away from where his gun would eject the empty shell and cocked his gun. Raising it, one marred, disfigured arm tense with bulging muscle, the other supporting, he looked over his shoulder at her...and fired.

He'd aimed previously, and his stance was so steady that the rounds he fired off hit their mark in a deadly, exacting fashion. He kept his obsidian gaze on Jane as he finished off his clip, and lowered his arms to turn and move closer, not bothering to examine his hits, as if he already knew he'd hit his mark.

Cundo rested one hand over Jane's shoulder, the heat from his arm practically singing the hair she'd pulled into her ballcap. Jane took in a deep breath and returned his steady gaze.

"I missed you this week."

The statement was so tender, it almost surprised her. But then again, Cundo was full of surprises. Instead of responding, she tipped her head back and cupped her hand around the back of his neck and pulled his lips to hers. Their kiss was just as electric as it had been the first time, but this time she knew what she had to look forward to.

As Cundo moved his mouth over hers, she wondered if this was the sensation everyone received when kissing, and if so, why didn't she feel that way when she'd seduced and played with experiments and victims in the past? Why had they felt like big, gaping fish giving her CPR? Cundo felt like he was placing a bolt of electricity directly into her mouth. And when they'd shared his bed...it seemed she'd grasped a lightning rod.

"No PDA in my range," Diego's distant, mocking voice roused them from their reverie. Cundo grunted in response and landed one more rough, possessive kiss on Jane's already swollen lips and turned back to the counter of his stall.

"Do you want to shoot my Beretta?" he asked, sounding about as out of breath as Jane.

"God yes," she said smilingly, and allowed him to put his arms around her to position her into the correct stance. Instead of stiffening as she would with any other person who'd enclosed their body around her, she went limp in his arms. She was practically giggling as he frustratedly repositioned her arms.

"You little..."

She laughed and leaned back into him as he tried to put her hands into the correct grip.

"You can't pretend you don't know what to do," he said into her ear with laughter in his voice.

"I can do whatever I want," she replied, nestling against his chest.

Cundo chuckled at that and gave up on her hold on the Beretta, raining kisses down on her neck. Jane tilted her head back and grinned as her world came together perfectly.

• • •

Cundo hadn't been able to let Jane go until around seven o'clock that evening. They'd driven around after the range until her hand on his thigh grew unavoidable, and they went back to the bar to do the things they couldn't in front of his friends.

Being with Jane felt so right and good that he didn't remember what he'd seen in her shed until he dropped her off. He left her on her front porch with her gun case and his t-shirt on her curvy little body, physically restraining himself from going into her house, lest he be tempted to stay the night and forget to go home and prep the brisket for tomorrow's lunch at the bar. She'd glowered at him in earnest for refusing to come in, the vicious look he often caught in her eyes translating into a feral pout. It was adorably characteristic of his odd lover and made it even harder for him to leave.

By the time he'd made it to the highway, his fuzzy, rose-tinted thoughts cleared enough that one name cut through the clouds-

Phillip Caruthers.

He had completely forgotten.

Cundo considered where he stood with Jane at this point. She may have seemed angry earlier, but perhaps it was a result of him invading her privacy- he could relate to that feeling. He wanted to talk to her about it, but he would seem psychotic showing up at her house just to bring up the private writing he'd violated earlier in the day.

Then he saw her backpack in the rear-view mirror.

It was sitting up, half-open from her digging around for a comb after he'd destroyed her ponytail during a make-out session. She'd left her ammo...clearly he needed to return it.

Before he could second-guess himself, Cundo made a u-turn right in the middle of the access road and drove back to Jane's cabin, only to find her truck missing.

Cundo sat for a few moments in her driveway, very still, until cat-paw droplets of rain appeared on his windshield. He took a breath and got out of the truck.

What the hell am I doing?

Snatching her backpack off the seat and rushing up to the front porch, he rummaged around, looking for a house key.

I'll just drop it inside the doorway and lock up. Nothing more.

But he didn't.

Instead of house keys, which must've been attached to her car keys, he found the unassuming ring of keys that she'd used to lock up the shed.

Don't do it.

But he did.

Under the cover of the rain, which began to fall more heavily, he tried out the different keys and found the two that unlocked the sturdy door. The combination was left to evade him.

What had the combination to her gun case been?

It worked.

With a soft click, the door yielded to him, and he entered the dry, still space with caution. Part of him thought the place might be rigged with traps for unwanted visitors such as himself.

Her desk remained untouched, the notepad still in place. He crept over to it and dried his hands on the cloth-covered chair before dropping into it and flipping through her notepad.

There was his name.

Not Phillip Caruther's...

His name.

His hands shook.

"Facundo Locklear" with his birthday, mother's name, and service information. She'd written a question mark next to his name and some scrawling thoughts. "Investigating me?" "Obstacle." "Avoid." "How to throw him off the scent?" She thought he was an obstacle? An obstacle to what?

As he continued to flip through the pages, he found more men's names and information, but they weren't written like his. They were written in charts- acronyms that he couldn't recognize labelling each column. With hesitation, he pulled his phone out and looked the names up on the internet, one by one.

Some of the names didn't produce any suspicious search results, but he managed to find several obituaries, and a couple of news articles. Had he come across these without the context of Jane's notepad, he wouldn't have thought anything of them. His pulse raced more and more as he read through them, his hands almost sweating too much to touch the pages.

"Nicholas Trejo, 43- a beloved son and brother. He went home to Our Lord and Savior on May 10th after suffering injuries from a car accident. He is preceded in death by…"

"Local authorities say that the victim's wallet, cell phone, and shoes were missing, suggesting a mugging gone wrong…"

"The deceased's family claims that Farrell's involvement in local gang activity had led to severe injuries in the past…"

With every word, Cundo's dread grew. Jane possessed a notepad full of information on dead men, and along with them sat his own.

There were clearly many more pages that had been ripped out, which prompted Cundo to begin looking frantically through the pages and stacks on the desk, through the drawer and through the boxes beside the desk. Most of it was paperwork for her father's cabin and the life insurance he'd left behind, but he managed to find a manilla envelope marked "for Jane". He wondered if there was anyone else involved in whatever it was she was doing.

Inside the envelope, he found a short list of typed information and a transcribed confession.

Her father's killer.

Something about holding this information felt wrong, more wrong than learning that Jane was somehow involved in the deaths of random men. Cundo wanted every detail from her lips, in her voice, her real voice, explaining to him how this information wound up in her hands, and for some reason, he also wanted to know how she felt about her father's murderer.

He should want to get out of that shed and leave, never to speak to her again, but he needed answers, and he wasn't going to get any invading her privacy further. In the notes she'd scrawled on one of the sheets, he found an address. Typing it into his GPS, he decided to investigate what it was exactly that she was doing before confronting her. He had to have the upper hand somehow or she would use that pretty little actress tone and explain it all away.

Taking her backpack with him, he flung himself into his truck and followed the directions on his phone, trying not to think about what he would find. Another strange man on the verge of a mysterious death? Jane, following? A lover's embrace? A revenge plot?

Nothing seemed to make sense when it came to Jane Fairweather, and Cundo was done being left in the dark.

CHAPTER 15

Giant Petrel, Macronectes giganteus

The thing about the southern parts of Texas, even in the west, was that the sun didn't set in the warmer months until about nine o'clock. It was getting low by the time Cundo arrived at a shabby but neat building labelled "Aunt Cookie's Diner", and his GPS said, "You have arrived at your destination." He had pulled into the parking lot with the expectation that he would ask someone questions and find out what the hell Jane was looking for in regards to her father's killer, but there under the rays of the setting sun was her truck. He recognized the older model, having looked for it to appear in front of his own parking lot plenty of times. Swerving quickly, he parked on the other side of a delivery truck that concealed his massive vehicle.

Through the front window, Jane's unmistakable copper-gold locks shown through the dusty glass. Cundo turned off his truck and leaned forward, trying to catch a glimpse of his lover. She was seated at the counter, sipping on a glass of tea. She'd taken off her hat and released the curls, but had kept her shooting clothes on. Jane always looked primed for some kind of show everywhere she went, so the unassuming jeans and black t-shirt she'd stolen from his drawer made this situation all the more suspicious to Cundo. What did this diner have to do with her father's killer?

Then she turned.

Her face turned up to greet the waitress that approached her, and Jane beamed at her, her face instantly transforming from pensive to welcoming, and Cundo almost felt jealous. Did she know this woman? He wanted to be the recipient of that radiant grin, he wanted her to smile at him and tell him that this was all in his head, that she was a reporter, that she was a writer, that she was anything but a strange woman with a perfect shot and a sinister connection to dead people.

Cundo hated himself in that moment for all of the desperate, conflicting feelings he possessed, but as the sun went down overhead, and he continued to sit in place watching her finish a slice of pie and glass after glass of tea, he grew more frustrated. He wanted honest answers, and even without her saying a word, she was making him feel insane for suspecting her of anything. If it weren't for the pictures on his phone's camera roll of the pages of her notepad, he would be able to convince himself that he'd dreamed the entire thing.

Finally, after a couple hours of developing a sore ass from sitting tense and still in his car, he decided to leave. He wouldn't get any answers by spying; he needed to confront her. He could do it in the morning after he'd processed this in a restless night of sleep. However, when he looked up after fishing around for his keys and restarting his truck, Jane was no longer in her seat at the counter. He waited, sitting…sitting…

Then she appeared in a flurry from the door near the kitchen.

What the hell?!

She flew out like a banshee and burst through the front door. He sank low in his seat, but she only had eyes for her own vehicle, climbing in and peeling out of the parking lot seconds later.

Cundo stared after her into the darkness.

Shit.

He put his car into reverse and chased the beat up pick-up into the night.

· · ·

Jane's heart hammered against her chest, and she had to refrain from reaching up to press it down. She needed both hands on the wheel in case she hydroplaned in a puddle that hadn't evaporated yet. She was reaching 90 mph, twenty over the limit, but on this road in this town, no one would think twice about it. Hell, even the cops were driving this fast if there were any, and the headlights on the vehicle in the distance behind her were too high to be a patrol car. It didn't matter anyhow, she needed to get closer to the car she'd seen leave earlier.

She'd visited the diner the day before, and she couldn't stop herself from doing it again. She needed to see Mel, to remind herself of the darkness that had led her to Zemsta.

But she'd also needed to know if Mel was okay. Part of Jane wanted revenge from Jacob Diaz, but part of her wanted this woman, this counterpart to herself, to live out her adulthood differently than Jane. Mel was sweet, different, and in no way deserving of the life Jane had lived. It wasn't fair that her father had borrowed money from the cartel. It wasn't fair that she had become responsible for him when he became ill.

And it wasn't fair that she had to borrow money from his former creditors to pay for his hospice bills.

Jane had feigned a trip to the ladies' room at the diner to eavesdrop on the conversation happening a few feet away in the kitchen. Mel had caught a glimpse of someone through the kitchen window and turned white as a sheet.

Jane couldn't leave it alone.

"You're cut off. I've been treating you good, and you've been acting like a bitch. You ain't gonna be able to pay me back any time soon, you're just lucky I'm not telling anyone you owe me."

"Please," Mel pleaded, her small voice growing desperate. "I'll act differently, I've just been upset, I'm worried about my dad-"

"You're a whore, whores can't act different."

"I-"

"Look, you're done. Don't bother me with your bullshit anymore, I don't give a fuck about your dad, and unless you figure out a way to start paying me back with real money and not a weak fuck by tomorrow, you ain't gettin anymore money from me."

There was complete silence after this, but Jane could see a man in jeans and boots exit the kitchen from her hiding place. There was a gun tucked into the back of his jeans.

She could hear Mel begin crying softly.

Jane's fingers turned white on the steering wheel. She needed to focus on the tail lights ahead of her so she didn't get mixed up if they hit more traffic, but all she could see was red.

Mel had been paying for more time with her father with her body and her slowly withering soul. There had been times in Jane's young adulthood as a teen in the foster system that she'd had to make the decision between a beating and a violation, between hunger and silence. She knew what making that decision felt like...it felt like no decision at all.

Jane knew that nothing good would come from her interference, she knew she should just let Mel fall into a bit of debt, watch her father meet his end, and move on with her life. That's what she should do.

But that's not what she was going to do.

They reached a neighboring town after a little while, and Jane practically crossed herself in thanks for filling up her tank. Texas towns didn't have short drives. Mel's creditor couldn't have thought anything of having a truck behind him on the drive- if you drove on a long, lone highway like this one, you were partners in the drive for a while. There was no getting off.

Jane breathed more heavily when he pulled off on an access road and turned under the bridge. There were beat-up, tagged buildings framed by seemingly abandoned railroad tracks. If Jane had painted a picture of where she thought a member of the cartel would lead her, this is what it would look like. She made sure to drop back a bit as he made his turns so that she seemed less suspicious. She couldn't seem too terribly conspicuous with another truck behind her. It was clear that they were both pick-ups, which fit right into the gradually-urbanizing town that obviously used to be agricultural, if the old feed store the car turned into was any indication. She drove past the entrance to the parking lot and moved further down the street to an old parking lot that had once required a toll and a ticket, but the entry gate had long since been removed. She pulled up close until her truck hugged the wall and hopped out, holstering one of the guns from her case and pocketing an extra clip. She reached back into her car and pulled long, black, nylon gloves out of a disposable pack and rolled them onto her hands. She then removed the extra eye protection she kept in her console and put them on.

She made her way silently and swiftly to the old feed store, not exercising the caution she'd practiced all these years. She wanted in. She wanted blood. She wanted to end the predator that was taking advantage of Mel.

A desperation to stop another woman from turning into a dark, empty husk like herself rose within her chest, and she walked faster.

She could be walking into a den of other cartel members. They could be storing contraband in the warehouse behind the feed store. They could be keeping people there in the midst of human trafficking.

She could be walking into anything.

These thoughts made her shake, but she couldn't stop herself. She was at the back entrance to the feed store. It was too late for plans. She was here to do what she did best- she'd been careful in her career thus far, she'd earned this one, chaotic outburst. If she left nothing behind, how would this be tracked to her?

She needed this.

Mel needed this.

These men took advantage of the vulnerable, they didn't deserve the lives they'd been granted with. Her father's murderer wasn't the vicious predator she'd been hoping to eradicate. These men could be.

And with that thought, she yanked on the door handle, found it to be locked, and fired a couple of rounds onto the lock as she stood to the side. The shots echoed throughout the tattered neighborhood, but nothing stirred just yet. She lifted one booted foot and kicked the mutilated door in. It didn't matter if she made noise now, everyone inside, and maybe even her, would be dead soon. No witnesses. Certainly no film, considering the fact that illegal activities were most likely taking place inside.

Raising her gun, she burst into the dimly lit interior. A man sat at a folding table with stacks of money in front of him. He was fumbling with the gun at his hip at the sudden violence to his door, but he didn't have enough time. Jane fired and he was shot in the temple. He fell backwards out of the chair, and two more men burst in through a swinging door, one with a gun raised, already firing.

Two more shots.

They both went down.

And she was only a foot into the entrance.

Her blood was so hot, she almost couldn't focus. She developed tunnel vision, and all she could see was the door the men had come through. None of the bodies on the floor looked like the man that had been tormenting Mel. She wanted him.

Through the door, there were plastic storage boxes lining the walls, and in one corner, old, packed-down bags of animal feed. But as far as the store went, that was it.

Everything else was illegal.

It smelled illegal, the air tasted illegal. She could feel in her bones that something bad was happening here, and when she examined the surfaces of the desks in the center of the room, she knew she was right.

She'd seen money-printing plates before. Her dad had taken pictures of some and used them as evidence in a money-laundering bust. The open case on the desk in front of her was like a glaring neon sign. Jane crept closer and her heart leapt into her throat as her vision finally cleared and realized that she was currently in the bowels of something more intricate that base, animalistic criminals preying on the weak. This was The Big Stuff.

"What the hell are you doing in here?"

Jane whipped around to see Mel's creditor standing in the doorway, alone. He looked furious but confused, and she could understand why. Three dead men and a strange, small woman wearing goggles and gloves in the midst of it did not bring to mind any familiar context.

That worked to her advantage.

Her blood went from simmering down and chilling under the ice-cold fear of what she'd walked into...straight back into the hot, boiling, splattering fury. Her vision went red once more, and all she could see in front of her was a disgusting animal that was salivating and licking its lips as it stalked weaker prey. This was her prey- she was it. She was the top of the food chain, she was the gatherer of energy, she was the apex.

All of these thoughts occurred within a single second.

Without blinking, she popped off a shot into his left kneecap. He dropped to the floor, but didn't relinquish the gun he'd withdrawn, so Jane strode closer and fired another round into his hand. His gun seemed to leap out of his grasp and he yelped. He didn't stay down for long, but Jane wasn't planning on keeping him alive for long.

As he rose to his good knee and cried out in frustration, leaning out to grab his gun, Jane removed the knife she'd stowed in her boot that morning and exchanged it for her gun in her dominant hand. She waited until the creature before her had gotten close to reaching his gun before sinking her knife into the shoulder of his good arm.

He howled and swung his bloody hand at her. She retrieved her knife from his flesh with a sucking sound and danced out of the way. He reached back for his gun, but she kicked it out of the way. She danced on the toes of her boots, giddy with adrenaline, in need of a fight with this man.

Hand-to-hand combat was always a bad idea. It left room for hair being pulled out, blood being drawn, energy being spent, and her being overcome. But right now, she was absolutely teeming with bloodlust.

He got a burst of energy and lunged forward, and all Jane had to do was angle the blade towards him and he impaled himself on it. As he dropped his jaw and let out a wail, Jane took the opportunity to pull the knife out and thrust it into his soft abdomen. It was difficult to find purchase in his buttery body and penetrate the bubble of his rippling stomach, but she pushed hard enough and did. He wailed again and shoved against her, fumbling with his hurt shoulder and hand, but she wasn't done. She gritted her teeth and pulled out her blade to plunge it into him again and again until she felt the saturation of his blood through her borrowed shirt. He was no longer strong enough to fight, sagging against her as she supported his considerable weight, slowly lowering him to the ground, clumsily finding new places to apply her weapon. She was so frenzied that she didn't pay attention to the wet warmth spreading over her body or the fact that tears had begun to fall from her eyes and fog her goggles, and she didn't pay attention to the dark figure that appeared in the doorway.

By the time Mel's tormentor was on the ground, someone else was standing in front of Jane, and her temple felt cold. She felt like she could sense everything around her and yet nothing set off any alarm bells in her head when the man in front of her started speaking to her.

She could taste the air around her in her mouth and feel the warmth of the blood through the nylon on her hands, but she couldn't hear a word he was saying. It sounded like they were underwater together, and through her goggles, she could see a face, but if you asked her to describe it, she wouldn't be able to.

She simply stared at the man. He seemed angry, repeating his questions louder. The gun at her temple pressed harder and it hurt but she didn't wince. Maybe it's my time to go, she considered distantly, no real substance attached to the thought.

The last time she felt this disoriented was when she finally learned how to turn her brain off when she was being molested. She would unfocus her eyes and check out, pretending not to be there, and after a while of practice, it became true. She would simply hover above her body and look up at the ceiling.

That's what she did now. She could hardly focus as the man knocked the knife out of her hand and grabbed her by her hair, digging the barrel of his gun into her head.

I shouldn't have gone so hard so fast, she thought with vague regret. She was crashing, coming down off her high. Her prey was gone, and she was drunk on the success of her kill. It was okay if he finished her off, really. What did she have left to do? Her father's murderer was on his way to his maker and Jane had nothing left to offer after this.

Facundo.

The name hit her like a ton of bricks, and her eyesight refocused. Cundo. Was she wondering what Cundo would think if her body was found with a hole in her head among dead cartel foot soldiers?

No.

The name hit her like a ton of bricks because he was there.

Then there was a pop.

A deafening pop, even with ear plugs pressed firmly into her ears. As the pop sounded, the shouting man in front of her disappeared. Well, not exactly disappeared, but rather, burst. Where the top of his head had been, there was suddenly nothing.

The pain disappeared from her temple and she wondered for a minute why she was struggling to see her attacker.

Her vision was red.

Not the kind of red from moments ago, but bright red and murky, like a film.

Blood.

Blood on her goggles.

Jane looked down to see the man with the gun on the floor. She wondered where her own gun and knife were. They didn't seem to be anywhere she could see, and they weren't in her hands. Her hands. One of her hands was full of something. She looked down. Her arm was lifting. Why was her arm moving without her trying?

"Jane!" a voice burst through the haze in her head. "Jane, come on!"

The voice sounded familiar. Her hand was still full. She opened her fingers, but something gripped them and pulled.

Cundo.

Cundo was in front of her, pulling her by the hand.

"Jane, we need to go! Now!"

Why are you here? She wanted to ask, but Cundo was holstering her gun for her and putting her knife in his boot and she wasn't strong enough to stand her ground when he pulled her soaked, gloved hand along. She wasn't even sure she wanted to.

Mel.

The young woman's face was in the back of her mind as she glided through the rooms, towed by Cundo. Jane looked at her surroundings as they moved through the room with the money.

"Wait," she said, clearing slightly and digging in her heels.

Cundo looked back at her like she was insane.

"This looks weird," she said simply, pulling her hand from his and quickly moving around the room, still numb. Cundo glanced around frantically at the carnage as if to say, weird? More like horrific?

"We need to take some of this."

"Take it where?" Cundo hollered, then shook his head frantically and reached for her again. Jane grabbed stacks of cash off the table- large bills. Then, thinking twice, she ran back to the room she'd decorated with gore and snatched up the case with the money plates. Her head might be stuffed with cotton, but she always had a plan.

Cundo retrieved her once again and pulled her, unrelenting, out of the building and out into the darkness. No sounds of sirens came from the distance. No stirring, no people shouting and coming into the streets. This was the cartel. Gunshots happened.

Before Jane could think, she was in her truck. Cundo stuffed her into her front seat and began speaking frantically, but Jane could only catch bits- she was crashing again. No more plans left to make, no more shots left to fire. Cundo strapped her in and took the case from her.

"-follow me-"

"-can't drive you-"

"-can't leave your truck here-"

"Fuck…"

And he disappeared. It wasn't until headlights appeared beside her truck that she realized he was parked next to her and gesturing for her to put the car in drive. She could do that.

She followed him onto the road and let his tail lights guide her into the night. She could follow. She could do that.

But everything else faded from her head.

CHAPTER 16

Great White Shark, Carcharoden carcharias

Cundo had seen many gruesome ways that a person could both survive and die of some kind of violence. He'd seen his own reflection after surviving an IED. He'd held dying friends in his arms and watched the light fade from their eyes. He'd had to leave them behind to save the ones that weren't in pieces. He'd turned grown men into sprays of red chunks, but this night, following Jane and walking in on the destruction she'd created...was unlike anything he'd ever seen before in his life.

When he arrived, bodies already littered the floor, but through that room, he saw a creature he couldn't recognize. Jane, with her golden curls pulled back tight, black gloves up to her elbows, her body bathed in claret, her face red with exertion and tears. Cundo couldn't get the image out of his mind. She looked like a beautiful monster, like some kind of war goddess. He knew in his heart that the bodies were her doing. The man holding the gun to her head was screaming about what she was there for, who she was working for. Jane didn't seem to hear or see him, and Cundo knew that if he didn't act, she would be gone soon. He hadn't killed since his time in the service, and this wouldn't just be a kill, but murder.

But there she was, beautiful and disturbing and covered in gore...and a primitive need to destroy the man pointing a gun at her rose in him so fast, he hardly had time to find a good angle before aiming. And then he raised his Beretta and blew the man's skull to bits.

Now, he was frantically checking his rearview mirror to ensure that Jane was following him and no one else was pulling out onto the road. Her car followed behind at a close distance, and the road was dark- he forced himself to pull in a breath and think calmly. His first thought was to call Diego- he'd seen death alongside him, and the impulse to share this burden with his friend was overwhelming, but he knew he couldn't invite any more eyes on Jane. He couldn't even be sure why he was helping her. Why had she taken the money and the plates? Is this why she had information about dead men- did she kill and steal from them?

The drive to Jane's cabin seemed to go on forever, and he felt sicker and sicker as he tried to justify what he'd seen in his head. Was she in trouble with the cartel? He couldn't rectify the woman he'd seen back in that warehouse with the one he knew. His Jane- the one he'd made love to, the one whose secrets and hidden vulnerability made her more real to him than anyone he'd ever met...he couldn't imagine her ever taking anything from anyone for material gain. Oddly, the killing didn't seem quite as repugnant to him as her using dead people for their material belongings. He simply wouldn't believe that that's what she was doing.

Either way, he would need answers, and he couldn't get them out of the close-lipped zombie in the truck behind him- he needed to clean her up and get her back to normal...whatever the hell that meant for her.

They pulled up to her cabin, and Cundo made sure to jump out of his truck quickly to check on her. She was sitting very still, staring at her steering wheel. Cundo reached into the truck to unbuckle her seatbelt and turn off the ignition, and he realized that she was staring at the blood smears her hands had made on the steering wheel.

"Hey," he said softly. He touched her damp shoulder. She remained expressionless. Alright then.

He hauled her into his arms and wrapped her legs around his waist to free an arm for the house keys. He sent up a prayer of thanks that she was as slight as she was.

In the dark cabin, Cundo wasted no time getting her into the bathroom. There was an old claw foot tub underneath a small, detachable shower head, and he placed her inside it without removing her clothes. He dropped the stopper in the drain and turned the faucet on.

"Stay here, I'll be right back, Jane," he said softly to the unmoving figure in the tub.

He stripped off his shirt and left it on the floor before rinsing his own arms, smudged with the blood from her body, under the faucet. He wanted everything off, all the filth from what he'd just seen. He found some cleaning supplies under her kitchen sink and took it to her truck. He scrubbed down anything she'd touched, anything he'd touched. He did the same to his own truck's interior out of paranoia, and stuffed the used paper towels and bleach wipes deep in a garbage bag that he then stuffed deep into the bin in her garage. Cundo realized that he didn't really know anything about her home, and slowed down in his cleaning to examine the interior.

Her cabin looked like a middle aged man had just moved out, and he very well may have. Jane hadn't changed much from the furniture and decor that she'd placed back in their respective locations. Boxes lay here and there, labeled with various handwritings. He hadn't had to consider what would happen to your home's contents if your parents died when you were a child. His grandparents had handled the packing of the meager possessions he and his mother had had when she'd been killed. Who had taken care of Jane's things? Had she been able to take them with her?

He thought about the life she'd lived as such a young woman- a murdered parent, one foster family after another, and after what he'd seen of her intimately...abuse. Thinking about those parts of her life made his chest tighten, but it was easier to reconcile her behavior that way. It made more sense. In the midst of his thoughts, he remembered the cash and the case she'd brought with her. He rushed back out to her truck to find them on the floor of the passenger side- disorganized wads of large bills and an unassuming metal case that looked sort of like a tackle box. Taking them inside, carefully -using a paper towel as a buffer between the handle and his fingerprints- and locking the trucks and the door behind him, he rushed the items into the kitchen before opening the case. It hadn't been locked when she took it with her, which was a blessing. No more damage needed to occur.

He swallowed hard and set the box in front of him on the kitchen counter, bracing himself. Cundo wasn't sure what he would find, but-

What the hell?

A glow lit up the back window, and he rushed to the pane to see a fire on the ground in the darkness. He flung open the back door.

"Jane?!"

The figure silhouetted against the fire in an in-ground pit turned to him. Jane, in complete, naked glory, stared back.

"What the hell are you doing?!"

She opened her mouth, but closed it again, looking confused. She pointed at the fire. He could see her jeans blackening in the fire, and smoldering scraps of the light, cotton shirt of his she'd worn rising up on the smoke billowing towards the sky. He walked over to bring her back to the house, and when he put his hands on her, he noticed that she was soaking wet. He sighed and pulled her into his arms, trying not to think about her state of undress.

"Cundo," she said in a small voice. She still sounded disoriented. Lifting her into his arms, he took her back to the bathroom.

"Jane, I'm going to need an explanation at some point."

Cundo had wound up climbing into the tub with her and lathering her up, draining and refilling the tub. There had been so much blood, and her soft little body was absolutely coated in it. The tangy, metallic scent clinging to everything in the bathroom, and he'd scrubbed until it smelled like bleach, her lavender candle, and the lemon-scented soap that he continued to pump into his hand and clean her with- as if cleaning her could erase what she'd done.

"I know," she replied, surprising him. "I wish it was easy to explain."

Her head leaned back against his chest, and her soft, smooth cheek caressed the scars on his chest.

"Have you ever done this before?"

"I think you know the answer to that."

They sat in silence for a few minutes, the only sound being that of the water sloshing as Cundo lifted handfuls of it to rinse the suds from her body. Finally, she continued.

"It's never been like this. I'm always more careful."

"Careful…" he repeated, tensing.

"Yeah. I'm good at it. I'm in and out really fast. I'm never even a suspect," she continued in a low, gentle voice. It was flat, though. Methodic.

"What…do you do?" he asked, knowing full well that he didn't want the answer.

She didn't respond at first, and placed her hand over his much larger one, scarred and trembling. She stilled him and rubbed her thumb comfortingly along his wrist.

"I kill people sometimes," she whispered.

He took in a breath at her comment, but he'd been bracing himself for it.

"Why?"

"Because they deserve it."

"Who are they?"

"Predators," she said quietly. "Rapists. Molesters. People who extort the vulnerable. Cowards." Her voice grew more firm with each word. "People that deserve to live die everyday, and people who prey on the weak walk around, alive, healthy...it's not fair."

The things she was saying should have scared him, but he understood. The tremor in her voice underlay a lifetime of fear, a lifetime of taking matters into her own hands and being responsible for herself.

"I understand," he whispered back, not wanting her to shut down again. He was terrified that she would slip away and never be solid again.

"No, you don't," she returned, quiet but fierce. "I'm not right. I'm messed up. I didn't smoke and drink and bury my memories like all the other kids. When I got molested, I thought about it all the time. After the first time I got raped, I wondered why. Why did he want to do that to me? What was wrong with me? What was wrong with him?"

To his shock, tears sprang to Cundo's eyes as he listened.

"Do you know that one in three women will be sexually assaulted at some point in their lives?"

"Yes..."

"One in three...and virtually no woman will escape their life without having been harassed at some point."

"I know...I'm so sorry."

"I guess I just decided that I wanted to even the odds," she said. "I guess I was tired of being prey." She paused. "Do you hate me?"

Her voice was so small, so raw, that he closed his eyes, not wanting the tidal wave of emotion that came with her question.

Cundo's heart wrenched, and he pulled her closer in the cooling water. As a man of God and a servant to his country, Cundo had never considered that he would have to decide how he felt about his lover's habit of killing someone. He thought he'd left the war behind in Iraq, but there was another one happening under his nose, and he had become wrapped up in it.

"No," he whispered back. He felt her let out a shuddering breath. "How have you done this all this time without getting caught?" he asked, needing to know more before he made any decisions.

"I'm smart," she replied simply. "Really, really smart. And honestly, no one looks twice at someone like me." She tilted her head up and looked up at him upside down. "Would you?"

I did, he wanted to say. He had. He'd noticed the stirring in her soul where everyone else was still, and he'd been frightened then. Somehow, knowing what made her different gave him peace, even as he washed a dead man's blood from her hair.

"I can't..." he started to say. "I mean, I don't know how you can do it. Killing changes you."

"It does," she responded, suddenly sounding decades older than she was. "It changes you irrevocably, and you have to learn to live with yourself after. I guess I always thought that I would get killed at some point and it wouldn't matter."

He breathed in a hiss and clutched her closer, his heart pounding harder at the thought of her demise than it did at the thought of her killing. He wasn't sure how he was doing this- listening and understanding and not freaking out, but for some reason, the image she was painting of herself seemed more real and understandable to him than any other. Cundo couldn't picture her graduating high school and moving on to become the woman she pretended to be- a mild-mannered counselor who'd managed to remain innocent despite her life and went home every night to a normal, empty house and didn't do anything illegal. The woman he held in his arms was beautiful- stunning, celestial even. She was a regular, human woman, but she was also a killer. A killer, an artist, an incredible shot, and as he'd come to find out, a fantastic lover. What would he do with all these parts of her? What could he do?

"Are you going to turn me in?" Jane asked, the question echoing his thoughts and turning the air around them much colder.

Cundo brushed wet locks of hair off her neck and to the side, kissing her temple gently.

"I don't know what you expect me to do," he responded quietly.

"I never wanted you mixed up in this," she admitted. "I wanted to chase you away so you would never have to get involved. I never expected to want to be with someone." She paused. "Men have always either terrified or repulsed me, and it didn't cross my mind that one day someone wouldn't. Now you're permanently entangled and it's my fault. I'm so sorry."

Cundo hadn't guessed that she would be apologetic. He'd figured that she would attempt to talk him out of bringing her violent little hobby to light. But here she was, resigned and accepting her fate.

"What do you think would happen to you? You know, based on what you've done."

"I don't know," she said in a faraway tone. "I could probably get away with an insanity plea...if I'm lucky. With my history and my reasoning, I don't think I'd get capital punishment. I don't think..."

"Do you think they'd ever let you out of prison?"

"Probably not."

"Why didn't you ever stop?"

"I wasn't done."

It was an eerie response, and Cundo was reluctant to ask for elaboration. He simply stared down at her body, folded into the tub and curled up on his lap, still. Her hair was still pushed to the side, and he could see marks on her neck- a couple of scars. They were round and dark, and Cundo realized where he'd seen scars like that before- on a fellow Marine that he'd served with in Iraq. During late nights on guard, the man had smoked cigarettes and pushed the smoldering ends into his arm to keep him awake and sharp when they were delirious with sleep deprivation. Cundo had thought the man was crazy, but what seemed crazier now was the thought of someone burning a child's neck with a cigarette, for any reason. He decided that he needed to know why Jane wasn't done.

"What was it exactly that you were waiting for?"

"I wanted to get rid of my dad's killer," she answered tensely, and then let out a long breath and sank against him, as if she had been carrying a great weight with that statement. "I wanted to kill him. He took my family from me. He was the catalyst for years of abuse, years of learning how to hate and fear people...I wanted to take everything from him like he took everything from me."

"Wanted?"

Jane took a moment to respond, and before she did, she pulled away from him and turned on his lap to face him, sloshing water and suds around. Cundo's heart wrenched at the exhausted, drawn expression she wore.

"He's dying." Of all the responses, Cundo hadn't expected that. "He's nearly dead, and I found out that he didn't want to kill my dad. In fact, he was supposed to kill me, too. What the hell do I do with that?"

Cundo didn't have an answer for her, and Jane was looking at him so hard, it seemed like she wanted one. He realized suddenly that Jane didn't live by the rest of the world's rules because she hadn't been raised by them. She could have decided to ignore her past or accept it and move on to be something she'd never seen in her own past, but how could he judge her for turning out this way? For finding solace from her despair and fear in matters that were as forbidden as that of the people who'd ruined her?

"What does this mean for you now?" This was one question that he desperately did want the answer to.

"I don't know...I feel like there's nothing left for me to do. I can't hurt my father's killer, because it's not the same. I built this...code. For myself. It was the only way I could stomach killing at first, even though I really wanted to do it. And killing Jacob Diaz would break it. This whole time I was preparing for this moment, everything I was doing was for this...and not only am I backing off from him, but I was protecting his daughter? I mean..."

"His daughter?"

"Yeah, Mel...I don't know, I guess I feel for her."

"So that's what tonight was about?"

"Yeah..." she looked at him suddenly. "Hey, how the hell did you find me tonight?"

He quirked his lips. Leave it to Jane to set up a crime scene that couldn't be traced back to her and still not question how he had followed her there.

"Guess you've been pretty out of it. I broke into your shed."

He expected her to be upset about that, but she simply blushed, and not in the false, purposeful way she did in front of others. This blush was unexpected and crept over her upturned nose. His pulse raced.

"So...you saw all my stuff then?"

"Yeah." he said. "I know about Phillip Caruthers."

"I swear I didn't know about your mom."

"What would you have done if you knew?"

"I wouldn't have bothered making it look like a suicide."

Cundo startled at that, but the sentiment touched him. "Is that the sort of person you usually..."

"Yes. People that make the world a nastier place whether they're locked up, doing community service, or under a restraining order...people that will probably do it again. And again."

Cundo swallowed hard. "Thank you." She looked at him with surprise.

"Don't thank me. Not when you don't approve of what I do."

"Of course I don't approve. Even if it wasn't illegal...shit, this is dangerous, Jane."

"I know," she said, rolling her eyes. "I've been doing it for years."

"Stop," he said. "Stop doing it." He didn't know why he was making this demand, or even where he felt his authority came from to do so, but he wanted to say it. Just to hear her response.

"What if I can't?" He hadn't considered that.

"There are other ways."

She cocked her head. "What do you mean?"

"Jane, do you know what happens to people after they die?"

"Not really."

"Me neither. So what if the things you do here, sending these men straight to their maker- what if that doesn't do anything? I mean what if it's not enough? At least, not enough for the people they've hurt."

She narrowed her eyes at him. Cundo shifted uncomfortably in the bathwater under her gaze.

"Explain."

"What if...what if instead of doing things this way, you destroyed them here...on earth. Ruining their reputations, taking evidence to the authorities, bringing their crimes to light. I know that the justice system doesn't always work, but you said it yourself- people are less sympathetic to a dead monster. Think about how vicious they could be to a living one if you gave them the chance."

"Monsters know how to manipulate, though,"

"So? What is their manipulation compared to you? You're a literal killer." Instead of flinching at that, she smirked and looked at him flatly.

"Jane, do you know what happens to sex offenders in prison?"

"Yeah...but that's only if they get there."

"Then maybe you should make sure they get there. Or at least make their life a living hell if they don't."

She was staring at him with wide-eyed interest. "How do I do that?"

Cundo stared at this woman, this naked, lovely woman, who was asking him for a way to satiate her lust for justice in a way that didn't involve bloodshed. He looked at her long and hard, wondering why he wasn't turning and running the other way. Perhaps this was it for him- the purpose he'd needed, the reality that was his and no one else's. Not the white picket fence family that so many had wanted for him when he came home from service...but this. Jane. Jane, sitting in front of him in a bathtub and plotting the demise of monsters. Jane painting on a drop cloth in the backyard. Jane waking up next to him in his loft, Jane standing next to him and shooting 600 yards next to him and meeting him hit for hit, Jane holding his gaze and asking him for help, finally relying on someone other than herself. Maybe this was it for him.

Maybe it was Jane.

Blood, killing, and all.

CHAPTER 17

Leopard Seal, Hydrurga leptonyx

Cundo had insisted that Jane pack up her necessities and stay at The Red Light for a few days. He said that it was because if they'd left any evidence at the crime scene, they'd send someone to find her. Jane didn't believe him, though. She thought that he was trying to keep an eye on her to make sure she didn't go off the rails. His response to her confessions had been miraculously controlled, and even in Jane's wildest imaginings, she hadn't thought that he would have done anything other than turn her ass over to the town's authorities. Instead, he didn't seem like he was going anywhere, much less going to do something that would harm her. Her safety seemed to be important to him.

Was it possible that the fate she'd assumed she'd suffer due to her proclivity for murder wasn't going to happen, and instead she could have something she'd never allowed herself to want- a future?

After packing up her things, including damning evidence, the things she'd taken from the feed store, and her guns, Cundo had packed her into her truck and sent her back to his loft. Part of her wanted to tell Cundo that she'd been doing this for years and didn't need any help, but another part of her wanted to relish in the fact that someone else was taking care of her. It had been so long since she'd been able to relax and not look over her shoulder, to be able to rely on someone else. She just wanted to enjoy it.

"Alright, here you go," Cundo was saying, placing her duffel bag on his bed and taking her rolling suitcase to his closet. "You can store your stuff in here. I'm sorry I don't have a lot of space, I keep things pretty minimal around here."

Jane let a small smile grace her mouth and watched him as he placed her things around his room, making space for her. She had felt sickeningly guilty at his acceptance of her before he knew about her life, but now that he knew and was still gently integrating her into his life, she didn't know what to think. Could he have feelings for her? The real her?

"I really appreciate this-" she started to say, but Cundo whipped around and grabbed her face.

"I'm not letting go of you anytime soon. You promised to change your lifestyle and be more safe, and I'm holding you to that."

She stared up at him and saw the truth of it in his eyes. His hands, large and calloused, were firm on either side of her face, and she could feel in his hold that he truly wasn't going to walk away. It was hard to accept that with the number of times foster families had walked in and out of her life, but she wanted to believe this right now, she had to.

He leaned down to her, watching her for permission, and once she closed her eyes in invitation, he grasped her around the waist and lifted her to his lips. She flailed and fumbled for purchase on his body, fighting gravity and gripping his waist with her thighs. His mouth claimed her again and again, and she let him. Eventually, he flung her duffel bag from his bed and lowered her to the mattress. Jane couldn't quite understand why he wanted to do this with her now, but she couldn't complain. Not when his hands were pulling apart her carefully-braided hair and running down the length of her body. The care with which he touched her was so foreign to her that every time he did, she nearly cried out with relief. She had never thought she could be with someone without cringing, but here she had gained a lover who made her feel beautiful, excited, and more than anything, at home.

"Jane," he murmured against her neck as he rained kisses along it on the way to her shoulder. She pulled his head back to her mouth, needing to feel his stubble and scars against her face.

"God," he sighed. "I'll never get enough of these lips, they look and taste like candy."

She giggled and nestled into his sheets beneath him, locking him against her with her legs.

"You know, you're pretty strong," he said.

"Yeah, you have to keep in shape if you're going to chase down predators." She stopped and cringed, waiting for him to pull away at the reminder, but he just chuckled and began removing her skirt. She let out a short, relieved breath and helped him unbuckle her serviceable belt. She had cobbled together an outfit out of functional items earlier, looking more like herself than she had in a long time. Cundo had surveyed her toned legs regardless of the scuffed boots they ended in. She liked that.

"I want to do this with you...for a long time," he suddenly said seriously.

She grinned at him mischievously. "Sounds good to me."

"No, I mean...I want to be with you. Like this. For as long as you'll have me. I meant it when I said I'm not going anywhere."

She stared at him, clad only in a paint-covered tank top and men's shallow-tread boots.

"Why?" she asked sincerely. "Why me?"

"Shit," he whispered, swallowing and moving to sit beside her on the bed. "I don't know. I mean I know why I want to be with you, but I have no idea when it became enough to overcome...this. I'm like you, my reality isn't the same as everyone else's, I wasn't meant for...I just...I just want to be with you. I don't know how else to explain it. I should be asking you why you want to be with me."

"What do you mean?" He gave Jane an incredulous look.

"People flinch when they look at me. I scare little kids."

"You don't scare me."

"Yeah, well, you kill people. Maybe I should be the one who's scared."

Jane huffed a laugh and continued, ignoring him. "You're beautiful. You make me feel beautiful, too. Besides, I don't really notice that kind of thing about people. I notice hands."

"Hands?"

"Yeah," she took one of his hands in both of hers. "You can tell a lot about a person by their hands."

"What do my hands say about me?"

"That you're an honest person, you don't take advantage of people...you're tough, strong, a hard worker, but really, really good in bed-"

"Okay," he interrupted, laughing. "You're such a little shit."

"Seriously, though, I could tell you were good when I met you. I felt comfortable with you."

Cundo pulled her hands towards him at that, and lifted her tank top over her head. She leaned down to take off her boots, but he pulled her back up and shook his head.

"Leave them on."

She let out a laugh, a belly laugh that didn't sound girlish or fake or idiotic, and he dove down to kiss her stomach and encircle her in his arms. It felt perfect and delicious, and they both relished every second of it.

Later that evening, Jane lay soaking in Cundo's steel bathtub against the enamel interior. The water was fabulously warm, and the muscles that had been clenched for the past twenty-four hours were slowly relaxing. Cundo had tossed some bath salts in and Jane had laughed that he'd had the lavender-scented crystals stored in his linen closet, but he silenced her with a kiss and disappeared to go make dinner. Now, the aroma drifted around her on steam, and she leaned her head back against the rolled-up towel he'd placed on the edge of his tub, and simply breathed. She hadn't done that in a while. It had been so easy to ignore other people, but with the man making biscuits and gravy in the kitchen downstairs, she couldn't avoid how she felt. She wanted to do something for him, too. Every time he made her feel comfortable, she felt the urge to do something that made him feel the same way. She got the feeling that he didn't often get that opportunity.

"Hey, beautiful," Cundo said, coming into the bathroom. He carried a plate of steaming biscuits, gravy thick with ground sausage glazing them. Jane pulled the stool next to the bathtub closer, and patted her slick knees, poking out of the water.

"Put those down and come sit on papa's lap."

Cundo barked out a laugh and placed the plate on a stool, moving to divest himself of his jeans.

"You're such a freak," he chuckled, but shifted her legs apart to make room for his giant body. The water rose to the brim, sloshing over the side a bit as he settled in before her, slipping his legs underneath her and raising her up until the crest of her breasts rose above the surface.

"Hey," she giggled, trying to settle back into the water, but before she could, Cundo dove for her breasts and licked the droplets of water from her nipples. She gasped and pulled him forward, but he pulled away.

"Before we get carried away, there's something we need to talk about." She pouted. "What are we going to do with the stuff you took from the men in the cartel?"

Jane noticed the tension around his eyes as he spoke and realized that this had been weighing on him.

"The money is for Mel."

"Who?"

"Esmerelda. Diaz. Jacob's daughter. I...I wanted to help her. She's drowning in debt from his hospice bills, and she needs some independence. That man...the one I stabbed. He was loaning her money in exchange for...well, it wasn't good. If I can do anything to help, it'll be good. She can get out of here once her dad passes and not come back. She won't have to deal with this shit anymore."

Cundo looked at her sadly and ran his hand up her arms. "That's kind of you. I wish someone like you could've been there when you were going through everything."

"Me, too. Anyway, the case has printing plates for counterfeit money."

"What?!" he exclaimed, dropping his hands in shock.

"Yeah. I don't know what to do with them yet."

"We need to take them to the authorities!"

"If we do that, it'll alert people to the fact that the killings weren't committed by rival criminals, if they've heard of them yet. The cartel usually keeps things under wraps, keeps the cops out of it."

Cundo creased his brow as if he hadn't considered that. Jane continued, "I was kind of considering planting them somewhere they'll find them...somewhere that makes them think they were stolen by people in their own branch."

"Why would you want to do that?!"

"So they can destroy each other. It's not like I don't know how to erase any way of it being traced back to me."

"Jane, that's extremely dangerous." The seriousness of his expression and the sea-sponge loofah in his hand created a comical contrast.

"I know, but once it's done, it'll all be done. I won't be involved anymore."

"Don't say it like that, like you're actually going to do it."

"I probably am."

"Jane, no." His voice was so firm, that Jane simply pressed her lips together.

"So what would you have me do instead?"

"I don't know yet."

"Well, it has to happen quickly. It's a bad idea to keep evidence around for too long."

Cundo leaned back and breathed in through his nose, closing his eyes. Jane was frustrated, too, but she couldn't express it to him, she didn't have the right. She'd dragged him into this by accident, and he was trying to help her. She had no idea how she could've had a future where she continued her scenes if she chose to do so- Cundo would lock her in his bedroom and never let her get into any trouble.

"Look...I'll figure something out. Don't stress about this, it's mine to deal with, not yours."

"No," he replied firmly. "I told you I'm in this with you, and I am. One hundred percent."

Just as she was relaxing under his words and the weight of his steady gaze, they both startled at the sound of someone shouting downstairs.

"Hello? Anyone home?"

Cundo rose up out of the tub in a wave of cascading water, his massive body taut with tensed muscle.

"Stay here," he said with no room for argument, throwing a towel around his waist and grabbing his Beretta off of his counter.

"Wait-"

But he was gone. Jane clambered out of the tub after him, unwilling to let him accost someone naked and angry by himself. She pulled on a robe hanging on the door and ran into his bedroom to find her gun case, which was endearingly stashed next to his own. Pulling out her Glock 40, she rushed down the stairs to find Cundo facing a red-faced Frank. Cundo turned around at the sound of her sigh of relief.

"Hey, sorry to scare you, I should've recognized his voice."

"I apologize if I interrupted anything," Frank said, smothering a grin and glancing between Jane's hastily-tied robe and the towel that Cundo was holding up with his unarmed hand.

"What's up, man?" Cundo asked impatiently.

"I just wanted to come by and drop off those things you were asking for. I know you said to bring them when I came in for work, but I was running errands. Now could you two rednecks put your guns away?"

"Thanks, you can uh, bring them in through the back."

"What did you ask him for?" Jane asked nosily as Frank disappeared to pull his truck around.

"Nothing, it's...it's a surprise."

"A surprise?"

"Yeah," he said gruffly. "Just go upstairs and put some clothes on before you flash my friend and I have to kill him."

Jane grinned and scampered back upstairs.

· · ·

Cundo had done well, he realized. He wanted Jane to realize that he was serious about being with her, partly so that she would reveal how serious she was, and partially so that she would keep up her end of the promise and stay out of danger and stop killing. He wanted her, but he couldn't stay with someone that could be put in jail or killed at any moment.

The surprise he'd had for Jane had caused her to jump up and down excitedly, and blink away tears she tried to hide from him. He had Frank pull his truck up to the service entrance to The Red Light and unload the things he'd brought from home. His wife used to be an art teacher before she moved on to work for the central office, and they'd needed to move her art studio equipment somewhere to make room for a nursery in their house. Cundo had obliged by asking for the materials and planning a space for Jane's work in an old conference room left behind from the building's library days. He'd tried to make it a private party room, but no one wanted to use it. It was the perfect space to spread out the drop cloths, stools, and easels that Frank unloaded from the back of his truck. Jane hopped around, moving boxes and assembling easels with uncontained joy.

"This is amazing! Frank, thank you so much! Cundo, what- when did you decide to do this?" He gave her a look that said they'd talk later, possibly even christen her new studio, and kissed her on the forehead before moving to shake Frank's hand and thank him.

"We talked about cost- how much for everything?"

"Dude," Frank said exasperatedly.

"I'm not taking this for free."

As they haggled, Jane ran to grab the crate of art supplies she'd insisted on bringing with her, ready to set up a new piece. When she returned to her new studio, Frank had disappeared, and Cundo was spreading out the drop clothes.

"You...are incredible," she said, dropping the crate and moving to put her arms around his waist.

"I didn't want you to keep having to paint outside. Is that the only box you brought? We brought more boxes of shoes than art stuff with us."

She giggled and pulled his face down to give him a quick kiss before retrieving a medium-sized canvas.

"What are you going to paint first in your new studio?"

She looked at him slyly. "You, naked. Now strip."

Cundo playfully pulled his shirt over his head, and by the time he'd placed it carefully on a stool, Jane had popped open a tube of oils and squirted it onto a large brush. When he turned around, Jane thrust out her brush and smeared a long, violet streak over his abdomen and snickered gleefully.

"What?!" Cundo exclaimed, jumping back. Jane flung paint from the brush at him and he reached for her. She danced out of the way and shrieked giddily. "That's not what I thought you meant!"

She laughed with abandon as her lover began to chase her around the studio until both of them wound up covered in paint and kisses.

CHAPTER 18

Jane, Homo sapien

It wasn't until around noon two days later that Cundo agreed to let Jane go back to her house on her own. She needed to retrieve some more things, and it was clear that after forty-eight hours of being in one another's personal space, she would have a hard time being away from him just to get them. She insisted that she would be fine packing things up on her own, and after not receiving any notifications about her alarms being set off, Cundo reluctantly agreed to let her go alone while he was stuck at work. Jane wondered how Cundo had seen her in the throes of what constituted as mass murder and still managed to worry about her personal safety. She was the danger.

With her, she brought the case of printing plates that Cundo had stashed in his gun safe until they decided what to do with them. She decided that she wanted to clear the case and plates of any potential prints or DNA and launch it into the deepest creek she could find. There was no way it could be traced back to her. They had haunted the news and people had reported the sounds of gunfire, but there was no report of an investigation into any gang or cartel violence, much less murder. She was in the clear, and more importantly, Cundo wouldn't be caught up in her entanglements anymore either.

More than anything, she wanted to divest herself of the lingering pieces of her last scene, find a way to give Mel the money she'd taken, and be done with it. She couldn't imagine how she'd start another scene, if she ever did again. What she was developing with Cundo was worth starting over for, and even though she had no idea who she was without her pain and the justice she thirsted for, she was willing to find out. For Cundo's sake.

She had a feeling that her father would have loved Cundo.

When she arrived at her cabin, she felt that something had changed. Maybe it was the fact that she'd spent several days living with another person for the first time in a long time. Maybe it was the peace she finally found looking at her parents' home, knowing that they were at rest and she could be now, too.

Or maybe it was the man looking in the window.

Shit.

She'd spoken too soon when she said she'd be fine going on her own.

Before she could pull her Glock from her hip, the man turned, and Jane recognized him. Her father's old friend shielded his eyes from the sun and raised a hand in greeting as if he hadn't just been creeping on her empty home. She carefully placed her gun in the console of her truck and stepped out.

"Afternoon, Officer Lasica," she greeted cheerfully in a light tone. She wanted him gone so she could get back to Cundo as quickly as possible, but if he was here, he needed something from her, and she'd have to go along for the ride and pretend that he didn't set her teeth on edge.

"Hey, pretty girl, I just wanted to check in with you."

"Well, I'm not in there," Jane said, letting out a laugh that she hoped sounded breezy. "My truck wasn't in the drive."

"Oh, I know, I just thought you might have been dropped off by that new man of yours."

Jane wrinkled her brow but kept a smile on her face. "My new man?"

"Yes, that Facundo. Facundo Del Sur. I heard that you've been staying with him," he said with a note of disapproval in his tone and a mock-fatherly raise of the eyebrow. Jane dropped her smile. She didn't like that Lasica not only knew this but had an opinion on it- as if his involvement in her life hadn't ended abruptly after her father's death.

"How did you know that?"

He shrugged. "Eyes everywhere, Janie." He chuckled and she grimaced at the nickname. "So are you going to let me in or what? I'd like to see what you've done with your father's place. You know if you ever need help moving things around, you can always call."

Jane reluctantly moved to unlock her front door and allow Lasica in. What conversation he thought he'd get out of her was beyond her, but if she could put her house plants in a box and throw out her perishable items in the fridge in the next twenty minutes, she wouldn't have to find out.

"That's okay, I'm not here much, and I'm not sure how long I'll be staying here anyway."

"Janie," he replied in a chastising tone as she busied herself in the kitchen, placing the miniature cacti from her kitchen window in a plastic tub. "I think you might be moving too fast with this boy."

"Don't worry about it," she answered shortly, the statement being the closest thing she could manage to "mind your damn business".

"Well, that's not what I'm here to talk to you about."

"Mmhm?" she merely hummed, not looking at him as she pulled a trash bag to her fridge to toss out all of the wilting produce she'd neglected in her days lavishing in Cundo's loft.

"I wanted to talk to you about Jacob Diaz."

Jane's skin prickled with awareness, and the back of her neck felt hot with Lasica's gaze.

"What about him?"

"Janie, that's your father's killer. You haven't brought his information to the authorities yet."

Jane schooled her expression into one of confusion and worry instead of the weary frustration she felt and turned.

"I know. I decided against it."

Lasica's dull eyes flashed with anger. "I know that this is difficult for you to accept, but you have information that could bring your father's killer to justice. You might not be thinking clearly right now–"

"I'm thinking very clearly," she interrupted, clearing her voice of faux indecision. "I don't want to turn Jacob Diaz in. He's dying. He has a daughter. She doesn't deserve to watch her father go on trial while he's on his deathbed. The few minutes it took for my own father to be murdered changed me for the rest of my life, and I will never be the catalyst for another woman's destruction that way, no matter how it might benefit me." Lasica looked like he was about to interrupt her, so she dropped the trash bag and lifted her hand to stop him. "Diaz will die soon. It won't matter what he did after that, but what will matter is what he leaves behind for his daughter. She has her whole life ahead of her. Someone has to stop the cycle. I won't make her miserable because I was."

To her surprise, Lasica seemed to go red with anger from his throat up to his forehead throughout her speech. Jane braced herself with his response, assuming that he would demand justice on behalf of her father. She'd already destroyed the manila file of information he'd brought her, and if he hadn't made a copy, she intended to use that as leverage- she wouldn't be used against Mel.

"You entitled-" Lasica blurted, and Jane lurched back. He settled himself a bit and seemed to pull back. "Listen, this is no time for you to become a humanitarian. Justice from the universe or God or whatever you think you'll be getting isn't good enough. You need to turn him in, do you understand?"

"No, I don't," she said slowly, her voice involuntarily dropping down to her most calm and dangerous tone. The kind her father had taught her to use by example. "Explain it to me."

"He needs to be brought in. Someone has to pay."

She simply watched him become more angry. He continued.

"If he doesn't, then-" he stopped himself. He took a shuddering breath. "Is this because you saw her?"

"Saw whom?" Jane asked, her voice still deadly. He wanted to think she was stupid, so she would be stupid.

"You know who...Esmerelda. I know you went to see her. You met her and decided to get a conscience about everything…"

"Did you find that out with your all-seeing eyes?"

"Dammit, Jane, don't get smart with me. Esmerelda Diaz isn't an innocent little girl, she's as dirty as her father was, involved with the cartel!" Jane could tell that he thought those words would shake her, cause her to change her tune and give in to his demands. She simply continued to watch him, her expression unchanging. She was no longer giving energy to her act. There was none left...she wanted to see what else he would say.

"Pretty girl, listen to me…" he tried a different tone, moving closer to her and reaching out to put his hands on her shoulders. Her lips curled and her gaze danced over him with repulsion in her eyes. He dropped his hands. "I have your best interests in mind...I promised to take care of you if anything happened to your father."

"When? When did you make that promise? And when did you follow through?"

"Just listen-"

"I think I'm done listening."

"Jane, please," he said, but she was walking away. "Jane, did Esmerelda give you anything?"

She stopped in her tracks.

"Give me anything?"

"Yes, anything to hold onto. Did she tell you to hold onto it, that it would help her? I know you relate to her, but if she gave you anything for safekeeping, something she said she'd come get later...it's best for both of you if you turn that over."

Jane stared at him. He was trying to keep his expectant expression at bay, remaining more curious than desperate, but Jane could see a bead of sweat emerge from his scalp to run down beneath his sagging jowls. The longer she stared, the more he fidgeted.

"Jane?"

"What would she have left with me?"

He gritted his teeth. "Anything. Anything at all."

"Be specific. We got to know each other...girls exchange stuff all the time."

"Janie," he bit out. "Did Esmerelda give you perhaps some money? Or maybe a box? It might've looked like an old lock box."

Jane went cold.

There was no way Lasica could know anything about the missing money and the case of printing plates just from his old buddies on the force. There was no way he would know any of the details of what had happened at the feed store when she killed the cartel members unless... unless he knew.

Unless he knew all of it.

Unless he was involved.

Unless he was dirty.

Unless he was with them.

Jane was proud of herself- despite the sweat that had broken out on her palms, her expression remained unchanged.

"No...why would she need to give me a box?"

Lasica narrowed his eyes and worked his jaw for a beat. Finally, he seemed to relax, but still blew a frustrated breath out of his nose.

"Let me worry about that. I just heard about some unsettling things...if you got close to her...I don't want you getting caught up in something you shouldn't."

"Like my father?"

"What?" he responded, seeming genuinely confused.

"You told me that my dad might have been involved in something illegal. That he might have started giving false leads and using inside knowledge to benefit the cartel. Remember that?"

"Of- of course, I-"

"Unless that wasn't true."

They locked eyes. There it was. She was calling him out- show your cards, she dared him silently. Tell me what you really know.

The only sound was the humming of the fridge and the cicadas in the trees outside.

"Why would I lie to you, Janie?" he said softly. His attempt at a gentle tone transported on vocal cords damaged by years of smoking grated on her nerves.

"I get the feeling that you've been lying for a long time," she returned, just as softly. Her dangerous voice was back, and she could finally see it affecting him. His ruddy complexion was worsening, his pupils dilating.

"Just tell me where the box is, Jane, and I'll let you have your silence about Diaz."

Never had she imagined a scenario where she was pitted against her father's best friend and she was forced to protect her father's killer. Never.

"What box?" she asked, and she couldn't help herself. Her lips twitched up.

That play at ignorance and the mocking tone beneath it was Lasica's undoing. His arms raised suddenly, and in his hand was his Taurus, a 9 mm, old, from his days on the force. She hadn't even seen him retrieve it from his holster. She forced herself not to flinch, but the little girl inside her burst into tears. This man had driven her to school on days her father had to go in early. This man had gone to lunch with her and her father on Sundays. This man had been family, and now she was on the other end of his gun. The last thread of nostalgia that held the innocence of her childhood together fractured and came apart.

She didn't bother begging, pleading, or pretending to be surprised. The time for that had passed. She simply put her hands out to her sides, palms facing him.

"That's right," he said harshly. "I thought so. Now give me the plates, and I'll make this quick."

She snorted. "You're not even going to pretend you'll let me live?"

"Why bother?" he spat, seeming disconcerted with her response. "I need those plates. You're not going to let me have them without a fight, so here you go."

"What percentage are they giving you for the transactions for retrieving the plates? Ten? Fifteen? You know they'll just kill you once they have them back, right?"

"Shut the hell up and lead me to them!"

He was unraveling.

"You're retired and you fucked up, you really think they're going to give you a free pass and pay you? God you're stupid-"

"Goddamn it, show me where the plates are or I'll shoot you and fucking ransack this place myself!"

As Lasica grew louder, Jane retreated into her special place, the one where she became razor-focused, and everything moved slower. She was in her living room. Behind her, the front door was open, the screen door opening and tapping back against the panel with the breeze. Her father's armchair rested to her left and his bookshelf to her right, and she felt like she was being sucked back into her decade-old memories once again.

Her father's voice.

Jacob Diaz, scared, holding a gun.

A shot being fired.

The door gaping open.

The bookshelf and the gun that rested on it, untouched, unreachable by her father's lifeless form.

She wasn't a child anymore.

And her father wasn't there.

She was alone.

But she'd been alone for quite a while now.

"Answer me, you little bitch!"

Her gaze zeroed in on the sweating, old man in front of her with wild eyes and a desperate expression.

"You really messed up," she said, her voice flat, and before he had a chance to reply, she shifted her weight mere inches to the right and slipped her fingers over the revolver that sat, eternally cocked, eternally loaded, placed there for her convenience in honor of her father's sacrifice for her safety, for her life.

And swung it to face Lasica.

That's the thing about Jane.

She didn't make the same mistakes that men like him did. She didn't wait around to explain herself or peacock for an audience. She didn't make shows of power or strength.

She just aimed and fired.

. . .

Hours later, Jane sat, curled up on Cundo's lap in her living room. He'd wrapped her up in a blanket and was rocking her back and forth as the police officer asked her questions.

They'd discovered Lasica's body after a hysterical phone call from a young woman in the house. That young woman had dropped her gun after Lasica's body dropped to the floor to leak blood onto her carpet, and retreated to her truck to pull on a pair of gloves and take the case of printing plates inside. The right hand of the corpse of Officer Lasica was raised to clasp around the handle and sides of the case before it was lowered back to the floor gently, and the case was stashed in the backseat of the truck he'd parked earlier behind her cabin.

Jane had calmly replaced her gloves in her console and returned to her cabin to call 911 and burst into tears, frantically begging for help, as her father's old friend had arrived at her home to threaten her with a gun, and she'd reacted in self defense. "Is he dead?!" "What do I do?!" "I've never shot anyone before!"

She'd called Cundo shortly after and he'd arrived before the police- the joys of rural West Texas. The bars were closer than the local precinct.

By the time the police got there, Cundo had pulled her outside and she'd begun to shed real tears. In Cundo's arms, she let herself break down, she let herself realize what this meant. The confusion, the regret, the questions, the emptiness at having nothing to give her closure, was disappearing.

She felt cold despite the ninety degree weather, and Cundo rubbed his hands up and down her arms as she stared unseeing out of her window, answering the officer's questions on painful breaths.

He'd wanted her to find and turn in the man who killed her father.

He'd wanted her to close up her father's case so there were no more questions, no more prying, so he could move on and get away with more, and nothing would be tied back to him.

He was crazy, frantic, saying things that didn't make sense.

Those were the things she said, and paired with her shaking body and the drying tears on her face, the police handled her gently and didn't second-guess her answers, not yet...merely taping everything off, taking pictures, extracting evidence. Once again, her home was a crime scene.

They couldn't possibly understand that the reason why she was shaken was because she was finally grieving. Because she was finally succumbing to the feeling of helplessness that her father's death had given her. Finally letting go and being the terrified, fourteen-year-old girl that had hunched over her father's corpse and wondered if her world would ever be pieced back together.

And because Cundo held her, she knew she could let go. She could fall apart because he was holding all the pieces in place, like a cast, ready to heal back together. She didn't want to forget or change or go numb again, she wanted to feel until she passed out so she could wake up next to Cundo and remake her future. She wanted to live again.

It simply took another dead body in her living room to make her feel that way.

• • •

And that was how Jane wound up packing away her things, repacking the boxes into the two trucks that were left outside her house when the police cars and coroner's van had driven away. That's how she wound up unscrewing the locks from the shed for whoever moved in next, and leaving everything else behind. She would let someone else handle the bookshelf, the armchair, the stained carpet. They were memories now, and she was okay with that. She had everything she needed- her mother's coral sweater, her father's guns, their family pictures. Everything else was replaceable.

The most irreplaceable thing was the man who was next to her, whose obsidian gaze and scarred smile reminded her that she was no longer alone in anything she did, no longer alone with her thoughts. A man whose hands were built to hold her own and would never harm her- a man who accepted her past and present and wanted desperately to be a part of her future.

She allowed herself to want love again, and it was that love that Jane and Cundo packed into boxes and loaded into their trucks. As they climbed into their respective driver's seats, they looked over at one another and turned their keys. Cundo revved his engine and winked, and Jane smiled.

EPILOGUE

He picked his way over the debris- blood splatter, chunks of drywall, shreds of paper. People spoke around him and cameras flashed. People surveyed the scene carefully, making sure that nothing was left unobserved. His eyes flickered over everything just like everyone else, but he was the only one looking for it.

Law enforcement crawled over the scene like ants on a picnic, looking for signs that the dead cartel members in this warehouse were hiding something else, something new. He on the other hand was looking for something else entirely- a slip up.

She was always careful, but he'd managed to catch her a couple of times. He relished in the artifacts each time- a journal he'd stolen from her college dorm, a broken hair tie with a couple strands of curls wrapped around it found at the scene of a crime, and lastly, a footprint. Smeared and shuffled around, but a footprint nonetheless, and he kept a picture of it in his safe.

He desperately needed another piece of evidence of her involvement. Something to tide him over until he could see her again on a stake out. He was salivating for it.

"Hey, we got another shell," a tech hollered in the back room. "It looks…"

He rushed into the room and stepped over to the alleged shell. He could tell from first glance that it was a different caliber than the other two types they'd found at the scene. With a thrill running down his spine, he placed his black docker over the shell and drew it to him, pretending to look around. When he bent low, one gloved hand discreetly covered the shell on the ground and collected it.

"I don't see anything," he said with faux irritation to the tech.

"Oh," the tech said, his brow furrowed as he looked around. "Sorry."

When he was alone in the room, he pulled the shell out and looked closely. This was not the caliber shot from the cartel members' guns, nor was it the caliber used to shoot them. The only gunshot wound that appeared any different was on the body with the most damage. Jane didn't shoot this caliber.

His fist clenched around the shell.

She had a partner.

ABOUT THE AUTHOR

E.M. Miller is an English teacher and novelist. She writes crime, historical, and dystopian fiction on her collection of typewriters. Her writing is often inspired by her bizarre and vivid nightmares. She lives near her family in South Texas with her beloved dog, Mr. Darcy.

Miller graduated from The University of Texas San Antonio with a degree in English Literature, and she is currently pursuing her Masters in Gifted and Talented Educational Psychology.

NOTE FROM THE AUTHOR

Word-of-mouth is crucial for any author to succeed. If you enjoyed *Apex*, please leave a review online—anywhere you are able. Even if it's just a sentence or two. It would make all the difference and would be very much appreciated.

Thanks!
E.M. Miller

We hope you enjoyed reading this title from:

BLACK ROSE writing™

www.blackrosewriting.com

Subscribe to our mailing list – *The Rosevine* – and receive **FREE** books, daily deals, and stay current with news about upcoming releases and our hottest authors.
Scan the QR code below to sign up.

Already a subscriber? Please accept a sincere thank you for being a fan of Black Rose Writing authors.

View other Black Rose Writing titles at www.blackrosewriting.com/books and use promo code **PRINT** to receive a **20% discount** when purchasing.

www.ingramcontent.com/pod-product-compliance
Ingram Content Group UK Ltd.
Pitfield, Milton Keynes, MK11 3LW, UK
UKHW040237250426
12048UKWH00040B/1554